CW01612746

Invitation to Paris

Danika Prasad

Published by Danika Prasad, 2024.

This is a work of fiction. Similarities to real people, places, or events are entirely coincidental.

INVITATION TO PARIS

First edition. September 14, 2024.

ISBN: 979-8227806079

Written by Danika Prasad.

Preface

Life is an intricate tapestry woven with threads of joy, sorrow, triumph, and challenge. As I pen down this preface, I'm reminded of the profound ways in which our personal experiences shape who we are and how we navigate the world around us. This book, inspired by the journey of my own family and the myriad emotions and events we've encountered, is a tribute to that journey—a testament to resilience, love, and the unyielding spirit that binds us together.

At the heart of this narrative is Amélie Dubois, a character drawn from the core of our familial experiences, portraying me, Danika Prasad, as this character. Amélie's story is not merely a reflection of fictional events but a mosaic of real emotions and trials that mirror our own. Through her eyes, readers will traverse the landscapes of personal growth, familial bonds, and the pursuit of dreams amidst life's uncertainties.

The book opens with Amélie's world being turned upside down by the passing of her beloved grandfather, Alain. His death sends ripples through her life, and the narrative follows her journey through grief, resilience, and eventual healing. As Amélie navigates her teenage years, grapples with personal loss, and confronts the challenges of growing up, the story delves into themes of family, perseverance, and self-discovery.

As Amélie matures, her brilliance shines through her passion for medicine, particularly in the field of ENT (Ear, Nose, and Throat). Her inventive spirit leads her to make groundbreaking advancements in surgical techniques, symbolizing her transformation from a grieving granddaughter to a pioneering surgeon. The narrative not only showcases her professional achievements but also emphasizes the importance of support from family and the strength derived from enduring relationships.

The book also touches upon the dynamic relationships within Amélie's family, including her complex interactions with her cousins, the support from her parents, and the evolving dynamics with her brother, Alex. The story highlights the importance of family in overcoming adversities and celebrates the enduring bonds that withstand the tests of time.

This narrative is deeply personal, reflecting the essence of our family's experiences and the lessons we've learned along the way. It is a celebration of the human spirit's capacity to heal, grow, and embrace the future with hope and determination. As you read through Amélie's journey, I hope you find echoes of your own experiences and a sense of connection to the universal themes of love, loss, and the pursuit of one's dreams.

Thank you for joining me on this journey. May this book resonate with you and inspire you to find strength in your own life's tapestry.

With gratitude,

Danika Prasad

Contents:

Prologue

Epilogue

Prologue:

The sun was shining brightly over Nice, casting long shadows over the lush gardens and charming villas. In one of these villas, a thirteen-year-old girl named Amélie Dubois sat in her room, surrounded by books, notes, and medical journals. Her brow furrowed in concentration, she carefully adjusted her violin on the desk beside her as she pored over a particularly complex medical text.

Down in the garden, Amélie's twin brother Alex was engrossed in his own world. The rhythmic thud of a football against the ground echoed through the garden as he practised his kicks with an intensity that matched his sister's studiousness. Alex was a football prodigy, and every kick, every manoeuvre was performed with precision and passion.

Inside the cosy living room, Isabelle and François Dubois were enjoying a rare moment of relaxation. Isabelle, with her knitting needles clicking softly, was working on a new scarf, while François sat beside her, eyes on the television but his mind clearly elsewhere.

Amélie, after hours of study, finally stumbled upon a breakthrough. "I've found it!" she exclaimed, her voice echoing through the villa. She had been researching a new cure for dysphasia, a condition that had fascinated her for months. With her discovery in hand, she rushed down to share the news with her parents, her excitement palpable.

But as she returned to her room to document her findings, she noticed an envelope on her desk that hadn't been there before. The envelope was neatly addressed to her in elegant handwriting she recognised immediately. She tore it open and read the contents with growing excitement.

"Maman! Papa!" Amélie called out, rushing back downstairs. "Look at this!"

Isabelle and François looked up from their activities as Amélie handed them the letter. Isabelle's eyes widened as she read aloud, "Dear

Amélie, Alex, Isabelle, and François, I hope this letter finds you well. I have booked plane tickets for you all to come and visit us in Paris. We are eagerly awaiting your arrival. Bien à vous, L'Oncle Henri."

"Paris!" Alex shouted, his face lighting up. He sprinted over, grabbing the letter from his mother to read it himself. "We're going to Paris!"

Isabelle and François exchanged glances, smiles spreading across their faces. "It looks like we'll be packing our bags," François said, his tone tinged with excitement.

The house quickly buzzed with activity as the Dubois family began preparing for their trip. Amélie carefully packed her medical journals, her violin, and her notebook filled with recipes and experiments. Alex, on the other hand, stuffed his bag with football gear and a few favourite books.

The day of the journey arrived swiftly. As they boarded the plane, Amélie couldn't help but feel a mixture of excitement and nervousness. It wasn't often they left Nice, and the thought of seeing her cousins in Paris filled her with both anticipation and dread.

The flight was smooth, and the family chatted animatedly, the twins sharing their hopes and plans for the visit. As the plane descended towards Paris, the sprawling city below looked like a beautiful tapestry of history and modernity intertwined.

Upon landing, they collected their luggage and made their way to the exit where a familiar face awaited them. "Bienvenue!" L'Oncle Henri screamed with pride, his arms wide open as he welcomed the Dubois family to Paris.

Amélie's Diary:

Cher Journal,

Aujourd'hui a été une journée extrêmement longue et émotionnellement éprouvante, et j'ai tant de choses à partager. Je sens que chaque instant, chaque interaction, chaque pensée doit être consignée pour que je puisse mieux comprendre tout ce qui se passe autour de moi et en moi. Je suis à Paris depuis quelques jours maintenant, et bien que cette ville soit magnifique et pleine de promesses, elle porte aussi des défis que je n'aurais jamais imaginés.

La journée a commencé assez paisiblement. Je me suis réveillée tôt, bien avant que le reste de la maison ne soit en mouvement. J'ai toujours aimé ces moments matinaux, où tout est calme et silencieux, où je peux entendre mes propres pensées sans les distractions de la journée. J'ai pris mon cahier de notes et me suis installée près de la fenêtre, regardant le lever du soleil sur les toits parisiens. Les premières lueurs de l'aube sont si inspirantes, presque comme une promesse de renouveau.

As the sun climbed higher, I heard the sounds of the household beginning to stir. I decided to make breakfast, hoping to start the day on a positive note. I love cooking, and it's one of the few things that always brings me joy. I made crêpes with fresh fruit and cream, a little treat for everyone. As I worked in the kitchen, I thought about my latest research on dysphasia and the potential cure I had been developing. It's so exciting to think that I might be able to help people with this condition someday.

However, the morning took a sour turn when Jasmine came into the kitchen. She looked at the crêpes I had made and immediately took credit for them. "Merci, Jasmine, pour ce délicieux petit-déjeuner," Henri said, smiling warmly at her. I didn't have the heart to correct him, and besides, I didn't want to start the day with a confrontation. Jasmine's need for validation and her constant undermining of my efforts is something I've come to expect, but it still hurts every time it happens.

After breakfast, Alex and I decided to go for a walk. I needed to clear my head and find some peace away from the house. We strolled through the streets of Paris, and despite the morning's events, I couldn't help but be enchanted by the city's beauty. The architecture, the bustling cafés, the scent of fresh bread from the boulangeries—it's all so different from Nice, but in a way that's both exciting and comforting.

"Amélie, look!" Alex pointed towards a small park where children were playing. "Let's sit for a while."

We found a bench and watched the children. Alex talked about football, as usual. He described his dreams of playing professionally and how he couldn't wait to show off his skills to our cousins. I listened, but my mind kept drifting back to the lab in Nice, to my research, and to the feeling of being overshadowed here in Paris.

L'après-midi, nous sommes retournés à la maison et j'ai décidé de jouer du violon pour me détendre. La musique a toujours été une échappatoire pour moi, un moyen de me perdre dans quelque chose de beau et de parfait. Mais, alors que je jouais, Élodie et James sont entrés en courant dans la pièce, riant et criant, interrompant ma performance. "Pourquoi joues-tu toujours ces chansons tristes, Amélie?" Élodie a demandé, ses yeux pétillants de malice. "Personne ne veut entendre ça!"

"Je joue ce qui me fait du bien," ai-je répondu doucement, essayant de ne pas montrer à quel point ses mots m'avaient blessée.

James, bien sûr, a ajouté son grain de sel. "Tu devrais apprendre à jouer des chansons cools. Peut-être que les gens commenceraient à t'aimer."

Their words stung, but I tried to brush them off. I know they're just children, but sometimes their cruelty feels deliberate. Henri entered the room a few moments later, sensing the tension. He hugged me tightly and whispered, "Ne les écoute pas, ma chérie. Ta musique est magnifique, tout comme toi."

The rest of the day passed in a blur of similar small conflicts and moments of solace. I spent some time reading in the garden, trying to immerse myself in a novel, but my mind kept wandering. The duality of Paris—the beauty of the city and the challenges of living here—was becoming more pronounced each day.

Dans la soirée, nous avons eu un grand dîner en famille. Jasmine avait préparé un festin, mais une fois de plus, elle a utilisé certaines de mes recettes. Henri a fait de son mieux pour inclure tout le monde dans la conversation, mais il était évident que Jasmine et les enfants de Paris avaient une dynamique différente. Alex, fidèle à lui-même, a essayé de me défendre quand il le pouvait, mais je pouvais voir qu'il ne voulait pas trop perturber l'équilibre fragile de notre séjour ici.

"Demain, nous irons visiter la Tour Eiffel," Henri a annoncé avec enthousiasme. Everyone cheered, and for a moment, I felt a spark of excitement too. Visiting one of the most iconic landmarks in the world should be thrilling, but I couldn't shake the feeling of being out of place.

As the night drew to a close, I retreated to my room, exhausted. I decided to write down everything in my journal, hoping that by putting my thoughts into words, I might find some clarity.

Cher Journal, je dois t'avouer que Paris est un endroit merveilleux, mais il est aussi rempli de défis. Jasmine continue de me traiter comme si je n'étais rien, et même si Henri essaie de compenser, ce n'est pas toujours suffisant. Les enfants, surtout James, peuvent être si méchants. Ils ne comprennent pas à quel point leurs mots peuvent faire mal.

Mais malgré tout cela, il y a des moments de beauté et de paix. Comme ce matin, quand j'ai regardé le lever du soleil sur Paris. Ou cet après-midi, en jouant du violon, même si cela n'a duré que quelques minutes avant d'être interrompue. Et bien sûr, il y a Henri, qui est toujours là pour me soutenir et m'encourager.

Je me demande souvent si je suis trop sensible, si je devrais simplement ignorer les commentaires et continuer à avancer. Mais c'est difficile quand on est constamment entouré de gens qui ne comprennent pas ou qui ne veulent pas comprendre.

My dream of becoming a doctor feels both closer and farther away here. Closer because I'm inspired by the vibrancy and opportunities of Paris, but farther because the constant undermining makes me doubt myself. I need to stay focused on my goals and remember why I started this journey in the first place.

Je sais que je suis capable de grandes choses. Je sais que ma passion pour la médecine et ma détermination finiront par porter leurs fruits. Mais parfois, la route semble si longue et semée d'embûches. Pourtant, je dois continuer, pour moi, pour mes rêves, et pour prouver à tous ceux qui doutent de moi que je peux réussir.

As I write this, I can hear the sounds of the city outside my window. The hum of traffic, the distant laughter of people walking by, the occasional honk of a horn. It's a symphony of life, a reminder that despite everything, the world keeps moving forward, and so must I.

Tonight, before I go to sleep, I'll play a little more on my violin. Maybe a piece that's uplifting and hopeful. Something to remind myself that there's beauty even in the midst of chaos. And tomorrow, when we visit the Eiffel Tower, I'll try to focus on the wonder of it all, rather than the challenges.

Paris is a test, but it's also an opportunity. I have to remember that. And with Henri's support, and my own inner strength, I know I can navigate whatever comes my way.

Bonne nuit, cher Journal. Merci de m'écouter, de me donner un espace pour exprimer mes pensées et mes sentiments. Demain est un nouveau jour, et avec lui vient la possibilité de nouvelles expériences et de nouveaux espoirs.

Avec amour et détermination,

Amélie

Chapter 1: Unequal Gifts:

The first day in Paris was a blend of excitement and unease for Amélie. She woke early, her internal clock still adjusted to her routine in Nice. Quietly, she made her way downstairs, the house still blanketed in a soft morning hush. In the kitchen, she found a collection of ingredients and decided to prepare lunch for everyone. Cooking had always been her way of expressing care, and today she chose to make fried rice and pain sans levain, hoping to bring a touch of home to their new surroundings.

The aroma of cooking soon filled the kitchen, a comforting blend of familiarity and warmth. Amélie worked meticulously, her movements practiced and precise, each step a small act of love. As she plated the food, she felt a sense of satisfaction, a fleeting moment of peace.

But the peace was short-lived. Jasmine entered the kitchen, her eyes immediately zeroing in on the spread of food. "Oh, Amélie, I see you've made lunch," she said with a smile that didn't quite reach her eyes. Before Amélie could respond, Jasmine called out to the rest of the family. "Everyone, lunch is ready!"

As the family gathered around the table, Jasmine continued, "I thought I'd try something different today. I hope you all enjoy it." She beamed at the table, taking credit for Amélie's hard work without a second thought. Amélie felt a pang of hurt but remained silent, not wanting to cause a scene.

Henri, always perceptive, gave Amélie a knowing look and a supportive smile. "Merci, Jasmine," he said, his eyes lingering on Amélie to let her know he understood.

The rest of the family, oblivious to the undercurrents, dug into the meal with enthusiasm. "This is delicious, maman!" Èlodie exclaimed, her eyes bright with excitement. "How did you make it?"

Jasmine launched into a detailed explanation of the recipe, embellishing and exaggerating her supposed efforts. Amélie forced a smile, her appetite fading as she listened to the falsehoods.

After breakfast, the family gathered in the living room. Henri had a surprise for the children. "I thought we could do a little shopping today," he announced, his eyes twinkling. "It's a special occasion having all of you here, and I want to treat you."

The children erupted in cheers, and soon they were off to explore the shops of Paris. Henri took them to a chic boutique, where the girls were immediately drawn to the racks of beautiful dresses and rows of makeup. Èlodie's eyes sparkled as she tried on dress after dress, twirling in front of the mirror. "I feel like a princess!" she declared, admiring herself.

Meanwhile, the boys gravitated towards the display of clothes and jewellery. Léon picked out a stylish jacket, and James found a necklace that caught his eye. Alex, always practical, chose a new pair of football boots.

Amélie, on the other hand, felt out of place. She wandered through the store, her eyes skimming over the racks without much interest. She was used to being overlooked, and today was no different. When it was her turn, Jasmine handed her a single pair of socks, dismissing her with a casual, "Here you go, Amélie."

Amélie accepted the socks with a quiet "merci," her heart heavy. She tried not to let the disappointment show, but it was hard to ignore the stark contrast between her meagre gift and the extravagant items her cousins had received.

Henri, noticing her subdued demeanour, approached her with a gentle smile. "Amélie, I have something special for you," he said, pulling out a beautifully wrapped package. Inside, Amélie found a delicate watch, a pair of high-quality headphones, and a lovely dress.

Her eyes widened in surprise. "Oncle Henri, this is too much," she protested, though her heart swelled with gratitude.

"Nonsense," Henri replied, placing a hand on her shoulder. "You deserve it, ma chérie. You are special, and I want you to know that."

Tears pricked at the corners of Amélie's eyes, and she hugged Henri tightly. "Merci, Oncle Henri. Thank you so much."

Back at the house, the excitement of the morning shopping trip began to settle. Jasmine, in her usual manner, took charge of the afternoon's activities. The boys were soon engrossed in their new clothes and jewellery, showing off their finds to each other, while Èlodie pranced around in her new dresses, delighted with her appearance.

Amélie retreated to her room, the headphones Henri had given her providing a welcome escape. She put on some music and lost herself in the melody, letting the rhythm wash away the morning's disappointments. For a while, the world outside faded, and she could simply be.

But the respite was short-lived. Jasmine's voice called her back to reality. "Amélie! Could you come downstairs, please?"

With a sigh, Amélie removed her headphones and made her way down to the kitchen. Jasmine was there, surrounded by ingredients and pots. "I need your help with dinner," she said, not bothering to look up.

Amélie nodded, slipping into the familiar role of assistant. She knew what was expected of her. As they worked, Jasmine gave instructions in a clipped tone, her usual warmth absent. Amélie did as she was told, her mind drifting back to her research and the discoveries she had made before their trip.

That evening, the family gathered around the dining table once more. The meal was a feast, with Jasmine proudly presenting dish after dish. Amélie recognized her own recipes in the spread: the fried rice, the pain sans levain, and several other dishes she had perfected over the years.

As the family praised Jasmine's culinary skills, Amélie felt a mix of pride and frustration. It was her hard work on display, but someone else was taking the credit. Only Henri, with his knowing eyes, offered her a silent gesture of recognition.

After dinner, Henri pulled Amélie aside. "You did a wonderful job today," he said softly. "Your cooking is truly exceptional."

"Merci, Oncle Henri," Amélie replied, her voice tinged with emotion. "It's just... sometimes it feels like no one notices."

"I notice," Henri said firmly. "And one day, everyone else will too."

Amélie nodded, holding onto his words like a lifeline. Despite the challenges, she knew she had a supporter in Henri, and that made all the difference.

As the night wore on, the family settled into their routines. The boys played with their new toys, Èlodie continued to admire herself in the mirror, and Jasmine basked in the praise of her supposed culinary prowess. Amélie, however, retreated to her room once more, this time with her new watch and headphones, gifts that symbolized someone's belief in her worth.

Before bed, she took out her notebook and began to write. The day's events, the mixture of joy and sorrow, the sense of being both seen and unseen—all of it poured onto the pages. Writing was her way of making sense of the world, a way to process her emotions and find clarity.

As she wrote, she made a promise to herself. No matter what challenges came her way, she would continue to pursue her dreams. She would become a doctor, and she would help people, just as she had always wanted. And one day, her hard work and dedication would be recognized, just as Henri had said.

For now, she would take each day as it came, finding strength in the small moments of joy and solace in her passions. She would navigate the complexities of her family dynamics with grace and resilience, holding onto the belief that she was capable of great things.

With that thought, Amélie closed her notebook and climbed into bed. She put on her headphones and listened to her favourite music, letting the soothing melodies lull her to sleep. As she drifted off, she dreamed of a future where her talents were acknowledged and her contributions valued. It was a dream she was determined to make a reality.

The next morning, Amélie woke with a renewed sense of purpose. She dressed in the new clothes Henri had given her, feeling a surge of confidence. Today would be a new beginning, another step towards achieving her goals.

Downstairs, the kitchen was already bustling with activity. Jasmine was preparing breakfast, and the boys were chattering excitedly about their plans for the day. Amélie joined them, greeting everyone with a smile.

Henri noticed her immediately. "Bonjour, Amélie. You look lovely today."

"Merci, Oncle Henri," Amélie replied, her heart warmed by his compliment.

As they sat down to eat, the conversation flowed easily. The family discussed their plans for exploring Paris, and Henri suggested they visit some of the city's famous landmarks. "We can start with the Louvre," he said, "and then perhaps take a walk along the Seine."

The children's eyes lit up with excitement, and even Amélie felt a flutter of anticipation. Visiting the Louvre had always been a dream of hers, a chance to see the art and history she had read so much about.

After breakfast, they set off for their day of adventure. The city was alive with energy, the streets bustling with people and the air filled with the scent of fresh pastries and blooming flowers. Amélie walked beside Henri, feeling a sense of camaraderie and support.

Amélie's Diary:

Dear Diary,

Today has been an emotional rollercoaster. Paris is a beautiful city, full of life and promises, but I have already felt the familiar sting of injustice following me here.

This morning, I woke up early, determined to bring a bit of Nice into our new home. I made fried rice and pain sans levain, my favorite dishes. The kitchen was filled with comforting aromas, and for a moment, I felt a great sense of satisfaction. Cooking calms me and gives me a sense of purpose. It's my way of expressing love and care for others.

Mais alors, tante Jasmine est entrée dans la cuisine. Elle a tout de suite pris le contrôle de la situation. "Oh, Amélie, je vois que tu as fait le petit-déjeuner," a-t-elle dit avec un sourire qui ne semblait pas sincère. Avant que je ne puisse répondre, elle a appelé tout le monde. "Tout le monde, le petit-déjeuner est prêt !"

When the family gathered around the table, Aunt Jasmine continued, "I thought I'd try something different today. I hope you all enjoy it." She took all the credit for my work without hesitation. It broke my heart, but I didn't want to create tension on our first morning here.

Uncle Henri noticed. He gave me a supportive smile that seemed to say, "I know the truth, and I'm proud of you." His recognition comforted me greatly, even if no one else seemed to realize the truth.

The rest of the family, oblivious to the real source of the meal, praised Aunt Jasmine's cooking. "This is delicious, maman!" Èlodie exclaimed, her face lighting up with joy. "How did you make it?"

Aunt Jasmine launched into a detailed and embellished explanation of the recipe, claiming my work as her own. I forced a smile, but inside, my appetite vanished. It was a small reminder of the many times I had felt invisible or unappreciated.

Après le petit-déjeuner, oncle Henri a annoncé une surprise : une sortie shopping. Les enfants étaient ravis, et leur excitation était contagieuse. Nous sommes partis explorer les boutiques de Paris, la ville vivante et pleine de possibilités.

Uncle Henri took us to a chic boutique, where the girls immediately gravitated towards the dresses and makeup. Èlodie tried on dress after dress, twirling in front of the mirror and exclaiming, "I feel like a princess!" It was clear she was in her element.

The boys, meanwhile, found their way to the clothes and jewelry sections. Léon picked out a stylish jacket that he modelled proudly, and James found a necklace that caught his eye. Alex, always practical, chose a new pair of football boots that he seemed genuinely pleased with.

Quand ce fut mon tour, tante Jasmine m'a tendu une simple paire de chaussettes. "Here you go, Amélie," she said, her tone dismissive. J'ai accepté avec un "merci" silencieux, ressentant la piqûre familière d'être négligée. C'était comme si mes besoins et mes désirs étaient une réflexion après coup, quelque chose à traiter de manière minimale et sans attention.

Mais alors, oncle Henri s'est approché de moi avec un sourire doux. "Amélie, j'ai quelque chose de spécial pour toi," a-t-il dit en me tendant un paquet joliment emballé. À l'intérieur, j'ai trouvé une montre délicate, un casque de haute qualité et une jolie robe.

"Oncle Henri, c'est trop," ai-je protesté, mon cœur gonflé de gratitude mais aussi accablé par sa générosité.

"Nonsense," he replied, placing a hand on my shoulder. "You deserve it, ma chérie. You are special, and I want you to know that."

Les larmes me sont montées aux yeux et je l'ai serré dans mes bras. "Merci, Oncle Henri. Merci beaucoup." Ses mots et son cadeau signifiaient plus pour moi que je ne pouvais l'exprimer.

Back at the house, the excitement from the shopping trip began to settle. Aunt Jasmine, as usual, took charge of the afternoon's activities. The boys were engrossed in their new clothes and jewelry, showing off their finds to each other, while Èlodie paraded around in her new dresses.

Je me suis retirée dans ma chambre, enfilant le casque qu'oncle Henri m'avait offert. La musique offrait une évasion bienvenue. Pendant un moment, le monde extérieur s'est estompé, et je pouvais simplement être.

Mais alors tante Jasmine m'a appelée en bas. "Amélie ! Pourrais-tu venir aider avec le dîner ?"

Avec un soupir, j'ai enlevé mon casque et me suis dirigée vers la cuisine. Tante Jasmine était entourée d'ingrédients et de casseroles. "J'ai besoin de ton aide pour le dîner," a-t-elle dit sans même lever les yeux.

I nodded and slipped into my usual role of assistant. We worked in silence, with her giving instructions and me following them. It was a familiar routine, one that I had grown accustomed to over the years. Cooking for the family had always been my responsibility, even if the credit rarely came my way.

As we worked, my thoughts wandered. I couldn't shake the feeling of being undervalued, of my contributions being overlooked. Why did it always have to be this way? Pourquoi ne pouvait-elle pas reconnaître mon travail, ne serait-ce qu'une fois ?

Dinner was finally ready, and we set the table together. The family gathered once more, and as usual, Aunt Jasmine took center stage, explaining the dishes and accepting the praise that was rightfully mine. I watched silently, feeling a mix of frustration and resignation.

Après le dîner, j'ai essayé de m'échapper dans ma chambre, mais Èlodie m'a arrêtée. "Amélie, viens jouer avec nous !" she insisted, her eyes bright with excitement.

I wanted to decline, to retreat into my own world, but I couldn't disappoint her. "D'accord, Èlodie," I said with a smile, following her to the living room where the boys were already setting up a game.

We played for a while, and despite my earlier frustrations, I found myself laughing and enjoying the moment. Èlodie has a way of bringing joy into any situation, and her enthusiasm was infectious. For a little while, I could forget about the injustices of the day and simply be a part of the family.

But as the evening wore on and the game ended, the weight of the day's events settled back on my shoulders. I returned to my room, exhausted both physically and emotionally. I put on my new headphones and let the music wash over me, finding solace in the familiar melodies.

Aujourd'hui, j'ai appris que même dans un nouvel environnement, les vieilles blessures peuvent suivre. Mais j'ai aussi appris que des moments de réconfort peuvent être trouvés dans les gestes de ceux qui nous aiment vraiment, comme oncle Henri. His kindness and understanding gave me strength, reminding me that I am valued, even if it doesn't always feel that way.

I will hold on to that thought as I face the days ahead in this new city. Paris may be full of challenges, but it is also full of possibilities. And as long as I have people like Uncle Henri by my side, I know I can navigate whatever comes my way.

Je t'écrirai demain, cher journal. Pour l'instant, je vais laisser la musique me bercer et m'apporter un peu de paix avant de dormir.

Avec tout mon amour,

Amélie

Chapter 2: Unwelcome Realizations:

The sun had barely risen when the Dubois household in Paris stirred with anticipation. Today was special—Grand-mère Marie and Grand-père Alain were arriving from Canada. Their visits were rare but always cherished, filled with stories, wisdom, and a sense of belonging that Amélie yearned for.

Isabelle and François, along with their children, had been preparing for this day for weeks. The house was spotless, the scent of freshly brewed coffee mingling with the aroma of croissants baking in the oven. Amélie had spent hours cleaning and organizing, ensuring everything was perfect for their grandparents.

Amélie woke early, her heart fluttering with excitement. She dressed quickly, choosing a simple but elegant outfit. "Today will be special," she whispered to herself, a hopeful smile on her lips. Her twin brother Alex was already downstairs, engrossed in a football game on TV, while their cousins Èlodie, Léon, and James were buzzing with excitement.

"Morning, Amélie!" Alex called out, not taking his eyes off the screen. "Excited for the grandparents?"

"Of course," Amélie replied, her voice tinged with anticipation. "It's been so long since we saw them."

Aunt Jasmine, their mother's sister, was in the kitchen, orchestrating the final touches for breakfast. "Amélie, dear, could you set the table?" she asked, not unkindly but with the authority of someone who expected obedience.

Amélie nodded and got to work, her movements quick and efficient. She loved her grandparents dearly and wanted everything to be perfect for their arrival. As she placed the last fork on the table, she heard the doorbell ring.

"They're here!" cried Èlodie, rushing to the door with the boys in tow.

Grand-mère Marie and Grand-père Alain stepped inside, bringing with them a wave of joy and nostalgia. "Bonjour, mes petits!" Grand-mère exclaimed, her eyes twinkling with happiness. She enveloped each grandchild in a warm hug, her love evident in every gesture.

"Bonjour, Mamie! Bonjour, Papy!" the children chorused, their faces glowing with happiness.

Amélie waited her turn, savoring the moment when she would feel her grandmother's comforting embrace. When it came, she felt a rush of warmth and security. "I missed you so much, Mamie," she whispered.

"Et moi aussi, ma chère," Grand-mère replied, her voice filled with emotion. "I've missed you all terribly."

Grand-père Alain ruffled Alex's hair and patted Amélie on the shoulder. "Look at you two, growing up so fast! How are my little geniuses?"

"Great, Papy!" Alex replied, his eyes shining with excitement. "I've been practicing my football, and Amélie's been busy with her medical studies."

Amélie smiled shyly, feeling a surge of pride. She adored her grandparents and their unwavering support. They had always encouraged her dreams, unlike Aunt Jasmine, who often overlooked her achievements.

The family settled around the breakfast table, laughter and conversation flowing freely. Amélie felt a sense of belonging she rarely experienced. But as the meal progressed, the familiar dynamics began to surface.

"Aunt Jasmine, this croissant is delicious!" Grand-mère praised, unaware that Amélie had been the one to bake them. Amélie opened her mouth to speak but closed it again, knowing it was futile. She had long grown accustomed to her aunt taking credit for her work.

After breakfast, the children were eager to show their grandparents their rooms and the various projects they had been working on. Amélie led Grand-mère Marie to her room, where she proudly displayed her latest medical journals and practice tools.

"Look, Mamie, Uncle Henri gave these to me yesterday," she said, her eyes shining with excitement. "Aren't they wonderful?"

Grand-mère Marie examined the tools with admiration. "Ils sont magnifiques, Amélie. You must be so proud."

"I am," Amélie replied softly. "Uncle Henri always knows exactly what I need."

They spent the rest of the morning chatting and catching up. Grand-mère Marie shared stories from Canada, describing the beautiful landscapes and their quiet life there. Amélie listened intently, hanging on to every word. She loved hearing about her grandparents' adventures and the wisdom they had gained over the years.

Meanwhile, downstairs, Aunt Jasmine was busy orchestrating lunch preparations. She called for Amélie to help, and with a sigh, Amélie excused herself from her grandparents and headed to the kitchen.

"Amélie, I need you to prepare the vegetables," Aunt Jasmine instructed, her tone brisk but not unkind. Amélie nodded and got to work, her hands moving skilfully as she chopped and sliced.

As they worked side by side, Aunt Jasmine began to talk about the upcoming family gathering, a tradition they held whenever their grandparents visited. "I want everything to be perfect," she said, more to herself than to Amélie. "This means a lot to them."

Amélie understood and put her best effort into the preparations. The kitchen was soon filled with the delicious smells of roasting meats, baking bread, and simmering sauces. Lunch was a grand affair, with the entire family gathered around the table, sharing stories and laughter.

During the meal, Grand-père Alain turned to Amélie. "So, Amélie, what have you been working on lately? I heard you're quite the little doctor."

Amélie blushed, glancing at Aunt Jasmine, who was already speaking. "Oh, she's been helping out in the kitchen, mostly," her aunt said dismissively. "She has a knack for it."

Grand-père Alain frowned slightly but didn't press the issue. Instead, he smiled warmly at Amélie. "I'm sure you're doing wonderful things, ma petite. I can't wait to see you become a brilliant doctor one day."

"Merci, Papy," Amélie replied, her voice barely above a whisper. She appreciated his support more than he knew.

After lunch, the family moved to the living room, where Grand-mère Marie and Grand-père Alain gave out the gifts they had brought from Canada. Èlodie squealed with delight as she unwrapped a beautiful dress, its fabric shimmering in the light. Léon received a new set of paints, perfect for his budding interest in art. James was overjoyed with his new book on football tactics.

When it was Amélie's turn, Grand-mère handed her a neatly wrapped package. Inside, Amélie found a set of medical journals and practice tools—the very ones she had always dreamed of having.

"These are for you, ma chère," Grand-mère said softly. "We know how much you love your studies."

Tears welled up in Amélie's eyes as she hugged her grandmother. "Merci, Mamie. These mean so much to me."

Uncle Henri, noticing Amélie's reaction, added, "You deserve them, Amélie. You work so hard, and we're all so proud of you."

"Thank you, Uncle Henri," Amélie replied, her heart swelling with gratitude. For a moment, she felt truly seen and appreciated.

The rest of the afternoon passed in a blur of conversations, laughter, and games. The children played together while the adults reminisced about old times. Amélie found herself drifting between the groups, enjoying the warmth and camaraderie that filled the house.

As the day turned to evening, Aunt Jasmine called everyone for dinner. The table was laden with delicious dishes, and the air was thick with the aroma of freshly baked bread and roasted vegetables. Amélie had helped prepare the meal, but as usual, Aunt Jasmine took the credit.

"This is wonderful, Jasmine," Grand-mère praised, tasting the fried rice. "You've outdone yourself."

Aunt Jasmine smiled, soaking in the compliments. "Thank you, Maman. I've been practicing."

Sitting quietly, Amélie felt a mix of frustration and resignation. Pourquoi est-ce toujours ainsi ? Pourquoi ne peut-elle pas reconnaître mon travail ? Uncle Henri, noticing her distress, squeezed her hand under the table, offering silent support. His kindness gave her a moment of comfort amidst the unfairness.

After dinner, the family gathered in the living room once more. Grand-mère Marie shared stories from her childhood, her voice weaving tales of a simpler time. Amélie listened intently, captivated by her grandmother's words. It was moments like these that she cherished the most—when the family was together, sharing their histories and creating new memories.

As the evening wore on, the children began to tire. Aunt Jasmine herded them upstairs, and soon the house was quiet except for the soft murmur of the adults' conversation. Amélie retreated to her room, her mind buzzing with the events of the day.

She put on the headphones Uncle Henri had given her and let the music wash over her, finding solace in the familiar melodies. For a while, the world outside faded, and she could simply be.

But as she prepared for bed, the weight of the day's events settled back on her shoulders. Today had been a reminder of both the love and the challenges that came with being part of this family. While she felt overlooked and unappreciated by some, the support of her grandparents and Uncle Henri gave her the strength to keep going.

Amélie's Diary:

Dear Diary,

Today has been a truly special and emotional day. Grand-mère Marie and Grand-père Alain arrived from Canada, bringing a warmth and comfort to our home that I had longed for. Their visits are rare but always cherished, and today was no exception.

La journée a commencé très tôt. The whole family was buzzing with excitement, each of us busy preparing for their arrival. The air was filled with the aromas of freshly brewed coffee and warm croissants—a quintessential Parisian morning. I could hear Aunt Jasmine bustling in the kitchen, making sure everything was perfect.

When they arrived, it felt like a breath of fresh air had filled the house. There were hugs, laughter, and tender words marking their first moments with us. J'adore mes grands-parents; leur soutien et leur amour inconditionnels signifient beaucoup pour moi. They enveloped us in warm embraces, their love and kindness evident in every gesture.

However, the day was also marked by moments of frustration. As always, Aunt Jasmine seemed to take credit for many things I had done, which reminded me how difficult it is to be recognized for my own efforts in this household. For example, she took full credit for the delicious breakfast of croissants and pain sans levain that I had prepared. It's hard not to feel overlooked and unappreciated, especially when I put so much effort into everything I do. I try not to let it affect me, but it's sometimes hard.

Grand-mère et Grand-père ont apporté des cadeaux merveilleux, y compris des outils médicaux et des journaux que j'avais toujours rêvé d'avoir. Their generosity and constant support remind me that my dreams are valid and that I am capable of achieving them, despite the obstacles I face. I was overwhelmed with gratitude, but part of me also felt it was too much. I don't want to seem ungrateful, but sometimes it's hard to accept such kindness when I'm so used to being overlooked.

Après un délicieux déjeuner, where once again Aunt Jasmine received praise for my cooking, we spent the afternoon talking and playing games together. Ces moments de camaraderie et de partage sont ceux que je chéris le plus. They make me feel a sense of belonging and love that I don't always experience. We laughed, reminisced about old times, and shared stories. Grand-père Alain even brought out his old photo albums, and we spent hours looking through pictures from when Papa and Uncle Henri were children.

One moment that stood out to me was when Grand-mère Marie pulled me aside to give me a special gift—an antique watch that had belonged to her mother. "Ceci est pour toi, ma chère Amélie," she said softly, placing it in my hand. "I want you to have it as a reminder of your heritage and the strong women who came before you."

I was deeply moved by her gesture. "Merci beaucoup, Grand-mère," I replied, my voice trembling with emotion. "I will treasure it always." Holding the watch, I felt a profound connection to my family's history and the women who had paved the way before me.

As the evening approached and the house grew quieter, I found myself reflecting on how lucky I am to have grandparents who believe in me so deeply. Aujourd'hui, j'ai appris que même dans les moments difficiles, l'amour et le soutien de ceux qui nous sont chers peuvent nous donner la force de continuer.

Before going to bed, I spent some time organizing my new medical tools and reading through the journals Grand-mère and Grand-père had given me. The more I read, the more excited I became about my future as a doctor. I can't wait to start using these tools to practice and learn new techniques. It feels like a dream come true.

Even with the challenges and frustrations, today reminded me that I am not alone. I have a family who loves me and believes in me, and that makes all the difference. Merci, Grand-mère et Grand-père, for reminding me of my worth and for always being there for me.

Bonne nuit, cher journal. Here's to more days like today, filled with love, laughter, and the unwavering support of family.

Love,

Amélie

Chapter 3: Unveiling the Shadows:

The following morning was one of those crisp, clear days that hinted at the lingering winter, but with the promise of spring on the horizon. The house was buzzing with the afterglow of Grand-mère Marie and Grand-père Alain's arrival. The warmth of their presence had permeated the household, creating an air of joy and anticipation. Amélie woke up early, her mind already whirring with excitement and plans for the day.

Amélie sat at her desk, flipping through the medical journals Grand-mère and Grand-père had brought her. She was deeply engrossed, her eyes scanning each page with a fervor that spoke to her passion. This was her escape, her sanctuary. The promise of discovering something new, something that could help others, filled her with an indescribable joy.

However, as the morning wore on, Amélie began to feel a sense of restlessness creeping in. Her thoughts became scattered, and she found it difficult to focus on the words in front of her. She closed her eyes, trying to center herself, but the buzzing in her mind only grew louder.

"Amélie, breakfast is ready!" her mother called from downstairs.

"Coming, Maman!" she replied, trying to shake off the unease that had settled over her.

Downstairs, the family was gathered around the breakfast table. The atmosphere was lively, with conversations overlapping and laughter filling the air. Amélie joined them, taking her seat between Alex and Grand-mère Marie. She tried to engage in the conversation, but her mind kept drifting.

"Amélie, are you okay?" Grand-mère asked, her eyes filled with concern.

"Oui, Grand-mère. Just a bit tired, that's all," Amélie replied, forcing a smile.

As the day progressed, Amélie's mood swung unpredictably. One moment she was filled with boundless energy, talking animatedly about her plans and dreams. The next, she was overcome by a wave of sadness, feeling an overwhelming sense of hopelessness. It was as if a storm was raging inside her, and she couldn't find a way to calm it.

In the afternoon, as the family gathered in the living room, Amélie found herself withdrawing. The noise and activity that had once brought her comfort now felt overwhelming. She excused herself and went upstairs to her room, seeking solace in the familiar surroundings.

As she sat on her bed, Amélie felt a surge of frustration. Pourquoi est-ce que je ressens cela? she wondered. She wanted to be happy, to enjoy the time with her grandparents, but her emotions were like a rollercoaster she couldn't control.

Just then, there was a gentle knock on her door. "Amélie, it's Grand-père. May I come in?"

"Oui, entrez, Grand-père," she replied, trying to compose herself.

Grand-père Alain entered the room and sat beside her on the bed. "You seem troubled, ma petite. Do you want to talk about it?"

Amélie hesitated, not sure how to put her feelings into words. "I don't know, Grand-père. I just feel... different. One moment I'm happy, and the next I'm sad. It's like I can't control my emotions."

Grand-père Alain nodded, his expression thoughtful. "You know, Amélie, it's okay to feel that way. Sometimes our minds can play tricks on us, making us feel things we don't understand. But it's important to talk about it, to let those who love you help you through it."

Amélie felt a tear slip down her cheek. "But what if I can't fix it? What if it just gets worse?"

"Then we'll face it together," Grand-père Alain said firmly. "You are not alone, Amélie. We are all here for you, and we will find a way to help you through this."

Later that evening, as the family gathered for dinner, Amélie felt a renewed sense of hope. She knew that her journey wouldn't be easy, but with the support of her family, she believed she could find her way through the darkness.

As they sat around the table, the conversation turned to their plans for the next day. "We should go to the museum," Grand-mère Marie suggested. "It's been a while since we've all gone together."

"Oui, ça serait merveilleux!" Amélie agreed, feeling a spark of excitement.

As the family continued to talk and laugh, Amélie felt a sense of calm wash over her. She knew there would be difficult days ahead, but she also knew that she was not alone. With her family by her side, she felt ready to face whatever challenges came her way.

Amélie's Diary:

Dear Diary,

Aujourd'hui a été encore plus étrange que hier. Les montagnes russes émotionnelles que j'ai ressenties semblaient s'intensifier, et j'ai l'impression de perdre pied. The day started off well enough, but as time went on, my emotions became more erratic and difficult to manage.

Le matin, j'ai décidé de profiter du calme avant que tout le monde se lève. I went to the kitchen to make myself some tea and found Grand-mère Marie already there, sipping her coffee and reading a book.

"Bonjour, Grand-mère," I greeted her, trying to sound cheerful.

"Bonjour, ma chère. How are you feeling today?" she asked, her eyes filled with concern.

"I'm okay," I lied, not wanting to worry her.

We chatted for a while about the book she was reading and my plans for the day. Talking to her always makes me feel better, even if just for a little while. She has a way of making me feel understood and loved, no matter what.

As the morning progressed, I tried to immerse myself in my studies, but my mind kept wandering. I felt restless and anxious, unable to concentrate on anything for more than a few minutes. It was incredibly frustrating.

Alex noticed my distress and tried to cheer me up by suggesting we play football in the backyard. Normally, I would have jumped at the chance, but today, I just couldn't muster the enthusiasm.

"Maybe later, Alex. I'm not feeling up to it right now," I told him.

"Okay, sis. Just let me know if you change your mind," he replied, giving me a reassuring smile.

Instead of playing football, I decided to go for a walk around the neighborhood. The fresh air and change of scenery usually help clear my mind. I walked for what felt like hours, letting my thoughts drift.

Part of me wished I could just keep walking and never come back, but I knew that wasn't the answer.

When I returned home, I found the family gathered in the living room, laughing and talking. The sight of their happiness made me feel even more isolated. I wanted to join them, to be part of the joy, but my emotions were all over the place.

As I watched them, I felt a sudden surge of anger. Pourquoi est-ce que je ressens cela? I didn't understand why I felt so disconnected and out of control. I tried to push the feeling aside, but it was like a storm inside me that wouldn't let up.

"Amélie, are you okay?" Henri asked, noticing my hesitation at the doorway.

"Oui, je vais bien," I replied quickly, forcing a smile.

I sat down on the couch, trying to engage in the conversation, but my mind kept drifting. Grand-père Alain must have noticed my discomfort because he suggested we take a walk together. I agreed, hoping it would help clear my mind.

As we walked, Grand-père talked about his childhood and the adventures he had with his siblings. His stories were always so vivid and full of life. I tried to focus on his words, but my thoughts kept pulling me away.

"Amélie, you seem far away," he said gently. "What's on your mind?"

"I don't know, Grand-père. It's like my emotions are on a rollercoaster, and I can't control them. One moment I'm happy, and the next I'm sad or angry. It's exhausting," I confessed.

"C'est normal de se sentir ainsi parfois," he said. "But it's important to talk about it and not keep it all inside. You have a family who loves you and wants to help."

I nodded, appreciating his words, but still feeling overwhelmed. We continued our walk in silence, each of us lost in our thoughts.

When we returned home, I felt a bit better, but the underlying unease was still there. The rest of the afternoon passed in a blur. I tried to keep myself busy, helping Maman in the kitchen and playing with the younger cousins. But the rollercoaster of emotions persisted, making it hard to fully engage in anything.

In the evening, we had a special family dinner to celebrate Grand-mère and Grand-père's visit. Maman made my favorite dish, ratatouille, and we all sat around the table, sharing stories and laughter. For a moment, I felt a sense of peace, surrounded by the people I love.

But then, out of nowhere, I was hit with a wave of sadness. I excused myself and went to my room, feeling like I was drowning. Pourquoi est-ce que je ressens cela? I wondered again. It didn't make any sense. I wanted to be happy and enjoy this time with my family, but my emotions were a tangled mess.

Just as I was about to close my door, there was a knock. "Amélie, it's Grand-mère. May I come in?"

"Oui, entrez, Grand-mère," I replied, trying to compose myself.

Grand-mère Marie entered the room and sat beside me on the bed. "You seem troubled, ma chère. Do you want to talk about it?"

I hesitated, not sure how to put my feelings into words. "I don't know, Grand-mère. I just feel... different. One moment I'm happy, and the next I'm sad. It's like I can't control my emotions."

Grand-mère nodded, her expression thoughtful. "You know, Amélie, it's okay to feel that way. Sometimes our minds can play tricks on us, making us feel things we don't understand. But it's important to talk about it, to let those who love you help you through it."

I felt a tear slip down my cheek. "But what if I can't fix it? What if it just gets worse?"

"Then we'll face it together," Grand-mère said firmly. "You are not alone, Amélie. We are all here for you, and we will find a way to help you through this."

Her words brought me some comfort. I knew that my journey wouldn't be easy, but with the support of my family, I believed I could find my way through the darkness.

After talking with Grand-mère, I felt a bit more hopeful. I knew there would be difficult days ahead, but I also knew that I was not alone. With my family by my side, I felt ready to face whatever challenges came my way.

Later that evening, as the family gathered in the living room, I felt a renewed sense of hope. The conversations were lively, and the room was filled with laughter. For the first time in a while, I felt a sense of belonging.

Chapter 4: A Day of Crisis

The morning sun filtered gently through the curtains of the Dubois household, casting a warm glow over the family as they gathered for breakfast. The house buzzed with activity as everyone prepared for another day in Paris. Amélie, still feeling the remnants of her emotional turmoil from the previous days, tried to focus on the positive. She was grateful for the presence of her grandparents, Marie and Alain, who had recently arrived from Canada. Their warmth and wisdom always brought a sense of stability to her life.

As they sat around the table, enjoying fresh croissants and pain au chocolat, the conversation flowed easily. Grand-mère Marie shared stories from their travels, and Grand-père Alain recounted humorous anecdotes from his childhood. Amélie felt herself relax, letting the familiar rhythm of family life wash over her.

"Amélie, your ratatouille was magnifique last night," Grand-père Alain said, smiling warmly at her. "You have a real talent in the kitchen."

"Merci, Grand-père," Amélie replied, feeling a flush of pride.

After breakfast, the family decided to spend the morning in the garden. The air was crisp and cool, a perfect contrast to the bright sunshine. Amélie and Alex played a light-hearted game of football, while the younger cousins chased each other around the yard. Grand-père Alain and Grand-mère Marie sat on a bench, enjoying the peaceful scene.

It was mid-morning when everything changed. Amélie was just about to score a goal when she heard a strange noise behind her. Turning around, she saw Grand-père Alain clutching his chest, his face contorted in pain. He staggered, then collapsed onto the grass.

"Grand-père!" Amélie screamed, rushing to his side. The rest of the family ran over, panic evident on their faces.

"Call an ambulance!" Isabelle shouted to François, who fumbled for his phone with shaking hands.

Amélie's mind raced. She had read about cardiac emergencies in her medical journals, but seeing it happen to someone she loved was a different experience altogether. She knelt beside Grand-père Alain, trying to stay calm. "Grand-père, can you hear me?"

His eyes were closed, his breathing shallow and erratic. Amélie knew she had to act quickly. She remembered the steps for CPR and took a deep breath, pushing her panic aside. Placing her hands on his chest, she began to administer chest compressions, counting aloud to keep herself focused.

"One, two, three..." Her voice trembled, but she forced herself to keep going. "Stay with us, Grand-père. Please, stay with us."

The minutes felt like hours. The rest of the family stood by, their expressions a mix of fear and helplessness. Henri knelt beside Amélie, offering quiet words of encouragement.

"You're doing great, Amélie. Keep going. The ambulance will be here soon."

Amélie's arms ached, but she didn't stop. She focused on the rhythm of the compressions, praying that it would be enough. Finally, she heard the distant wail of sirens. Moments later, the paramedics arrived, taking over from Amélie with practiced efficiency.

"Please, save him," Amélie whispered, her voice breaking.

One of the paramedics nodded, giving her a reassuring smile. "We'll do everything we can."

As the paramedics worked on stabilizing Grand-père Alain, Amélie felt a wave of exhaustion wash over her. She stood up, her legs unsteady, and stumbled back a few steps. The adrenaline that had kept her going was fading, leaving her feeling drained and vulnerable.

Isabelle wrapped her arms around Amélie, pulling her close. "You were amazing, sweetheart. You saved his life."

Amélie nodded, but her mind was already starting to spiral. The reality of what had just happened hit her like a tidal wave, and she felt the familiar grip of a panic attack tightening around her chest. Her breaths became rapid and shallow, her vision narrowing.

"I... I need to go," she gasped, pulling away from Isabelle's embrace.

"Amélie, wait," Alex called after her, but she was already running towards the house.

She burst through the front door, her heart pounding in her chest. She barely made it to her room before collapsing onto her bed, the tears flowing freely now. She felt like she was suffocating, the weight of the morning's events pressing down on her. The room spun around her, and she clutched at her chest, trying to steady her breathing.

"Calm down, Amélie. Breathe. Just breathe," she whispered to herself, rocking back and forth.

But the panic was relentless, each breath a struggle. She closed her eyes, trying to focus on something, anything, to ground herself. She thought of Grand-père Alain, of his kind eyes and warm smile. She couldn't lose him. The thought of life without him was too much to bear.

Minutes felt like hours as she fought to regain control. Finally, her breathing began to slow, the tightness in her chest easing. She lay there, exhausted and drained, staring up at the ceiling. She knew she needed to be strong for her family, but in that moment, all she could do was let the tears flow.

After what felt like an eternity, there was a soft knock on her door. "Amélie, it's Grand-mère. Can I come in?"

"Oui, Grand-mère," Amélie replied, her voice barely above a whisper.

Grand-mère Marie entered the room and sat beside Amélie on the bed. She didn't say anything, just held Amélie's hand, offering silent support. The warmth of her touch was a comfort, and Amélie felt a flicker of calm.

"You did everything right, ma chère," Grand-mère said softly. "You were so brave."

"I was so scared, Grand-mère," Amélie admitted, her voice trembling. "I thought we were going to lose him."

"But we didn't, thanks to you," Grand-mère replied. "You gave him a fighting chance."

Amélie nodded, the weight of the morning's events still heavy on her shoulders. "What if I couldn't have helped him? What if..."

"Don't think like that," Grand-mère interrupted gently. "You did everything you could, and that's what matters. You were there for him when he needed you most."

As the afternoon turned to evening, the family gathered anxiously, awaiting news from the hospital. The house was unusually quiet, the usual hum of activity replaced by a tense silence. Amélie tried to stay positive, but the uncertainty gnawed at her.

Finally, François's phone rang, breaking the silence. He answered it quickly, his expression tense. "Yes, this is François Dubois... Yes, I understand... Thank you."

He hung up and turned to the family, a look of relief on his face. "Grand-père Alain is stable. They're keeping him for observation, but it looks like he's going to be okay."

A collective sigh of relief swept through the room. Tears of joy and relief flowed freely, and the family embraced, grateful for the good news. Amélie felt a weight lift from her shoulders, her heart swelling with gratitude.

"Thank you, Amélie," Henri said, pulling her into a hug. "You were incredible today. You saved his life."

Amélie hugged him back, tears streaming down her face. "I just did what I had to do. I couldn't let anything happen to him."

The rest of the evening passed in a blur of emotions. The family stayed close, supporting each other through the uncertainty. Amélie felt a sense of unity, a bond that had been strengthened by the day's events. She knew that no matter what, they would face it together.

As she lay in bed that night, Amélie reflected on the day. The fear and panic were still fresh in her mind, but so was the love and support of her family. She knew that the road ahead might be difficult, but she felt a renewed sense of hope. With her family by her side, she believed she could face whatever challenges came her way.

Amélie's Diary

Cher journal,

Aujourd'hui a été une journée pleine d'émotions. Je me suis réveillée encore sous le choc de ce qui s'est passé hier avec Grand-père Alain. Le souvenir de lui, allongé sur le sol, m'a hantée toute la nuit. Pourtant, ce matin, je savais que je devais être forte pour ma famille.

I got up early and headed downstairs, the aroma of fresh coffee and croissants filling the air. Grand-mère Marie avait déjà préparé le petit-déjeuner pour tout le monde. C'était apaisant de voir ma famille rassemblée autour de la table, même si l'inquiétude pour Grand-père Alain pesait lourdement sur nos cœurs.

As we sat together, I couldn't help but think about the events of yesterday. Seeing Grand-père Alain collapse was terrifying, but I'm grateful that I was able to help him. Je me suis sentie si impuissante, mais en même temps, j'ai su que je devais agir rapidement. Les cours de premiers secours que j'ai suivis m'ont vraiment aidée, et je suis fière d'avoir pu appliquer ce que j'ai appris.

Après le petit-déjeuner, nous avons reçu un appel de l'hôpital. Les médecins ont dit que Grand-père Alain se rétablissait bien. C'était un énorme soulagement pour nous tous. Henri était tellement reconnaissant pour ce que j'avais fait. Il m'a dit, "Tu es notre héroïne, Amélie." Même si ça me fait plaisir de l'entendre, je ne me sens pas comme une héroïne. J'ai juste fait ce qui devait être fait.

We decided to spend the day at home, giving ourselves time to process everything that happened. Alex suggested we play a board game to take our minds off things, so we chose Monopoly. It was a nice distraction, and for a little while, we were able to laugh and enjoy each other's company. Léon et James ont été particulièrement compétitifs, mais c'était amusant de les voir se taquiner gentiment.

Later in the afternoon, Grand-mère Marie and Grand-père Alain came home from the hospital. Seeing him walk through the door was such a relief. Nous l'avons tous accueilli avec des câlins et des larmes de joie. He looked tired but happy to be home. He thanked me again for what I did, and I couldn't help but tear up. "C'était rien, Grand-père," I said, hugging him tightly. "Je t'aime tellement."

Grand-mère Marie prepared a special dinner to celebrate Grand-père Alain's return. She made his favorite dish, coq au vin, and I helped her in the kitchen. Pendant que nous cuisinions, elle m'a raconté des histoires de leur jeunesse en France et de leur vie au Canada. C'était fascinant d'entendre ces récits, et ça m'a fait réaliser à quel point ils ont vécu des choses incroyables ensemble.

Dinner was wonderful. Everyone was in high spirits, and the atmosphere was warm and joyful. We shared stories, laughed, and enjoyed each other's company. It felt like a true celebration of life and family. Après le dîner, nous avons tous pris un moment pour exprimer notre gratitude. "Merci à chacun d'entre vous pour votre amour et votre soutien," a dit Grand-père Alain. "Je suis tellement reconnaissant d'avoir une famille aussi merveilleuse."

After dinner, I felt a wave of exhaustion hit me. Les émotions de la journée m'ont vraiment épuisée. I decided to take a walk in the garden to clear my mind. The night was cool and peaceful, and the stars shone brightly above. I found a quiet spot and sat down, reflecting on everything that had happened.

It's strange how life can change in an instant. Yesterday, I was filled with fear and uncertainty, but today, I feel a sense of calm and gratitude. J'ai appris que la vie est précieuse et fragile, et qu'il faut apprécier chaque moment. I also realized how strong and resilient we can be when we face challenges together.

En pensant à l'avenir, je me sens déterminée à continuer à apprendre et à grandir. Je veux être une meilleure personne, pour moi-même et pour ma famille. I want to pursue my dreams of becoming a doctor and helping others, just as I helped Grand-père

Alain. This experience has shown me the importance of knowledge, courage, and love.

As I headed back inside, I felt a sense of peace. I knew that whatever challenges lay ahead, I would face them with the support of my family. Nous sommes plus forts ensemble, et je suis reconnaissante pour l'amour et le soutien que nous partageons.

Bonne nuit, cher journal. Merci de m'avoir permis de partager mes pensées et mes sentiments. Je me sens un peu plus légère maintenant. Jusqu'à demain.

Avec tout mon amour,

Amélie

Chapter 5: Farewell and Hidden Sorrows

The morning of January 23rd dawned bright and clear, a stark contrast to the turbulent emotions that lingered in the Dubois household. The time had come for François, Isabelle, Alex, and Amélie to return to Nice. The previous days had been a whirlwind of events, and though there was a sense of relief that Grand-père Alain was recovering, the family had to return to their routine.

Amélie felt a mix of relief and sadness as she prepared to leave. The house, which had been filled with warmth and laughter, would soon fall silent. The thought of saying goodbye to her grandparents and Henri was difficult, especially after the emotional rollercoaster of the past few days.

The house was buzzing with activity as everyone packed their bags. Isabelle and François were busy organizing a taxi to the airport, while Alex was in his room, collecting his things. Amélie was in her room, quietly packing her belongings. Despite the bustling atmosphere, she felt isolated and withdrawn.

Just as she was finishing up, she heard a group of voices coming from the hallway. Curious, she paused and listened, only to recognize the voices of Alex, James, Lèon, and Èlodie, along with Jasmine's distinct tone. They were standing just outside her door, their voices muffled but clearly audible.

"Did you see Amélie's face? It's like she's trying to act all brave," Jasmine's voice sneered. "She's just a show-off, thinking she's so important because she saved Grand-père."

"Yeah, she's always acting like she's better than everyone else," Èlodie chimed in. "Like she's some kind of genius or something."

"Seriously," James added, "why does she get so much attention? It's not like she did anything extraordinary. She just happened to be there."

Lèon's voice followed, filled with derision. "I can't stand how she always tries to make everything about her. She's such a drama queen."

Amélie's heart sank as she heard their words. The sting of their criticism was like a physical blow. Tears welled up in her eyes, and she felt a deep ache in her chest. The whispers that had once been just background noise now felt like daggers aimed directly at her heart.

Trying to hold back her tears, Amélie quickly finished packing her things and fled to her room. She threw her suitcase onto the bed and shut the door behind her. Once inside, she collapsed onto her bed, her emotions breaking free.

To distract herself, Amélie grabbed a tub of ice cream from the freezer and began eating it straight from the container. The cold, creamy sweetness did little to soothe her inner turmoil, but it was a small comfort in the midst of her distress. She pulled up a medical documentary on her laptop, hoping that the familiar, scientific voices would help ground her.

But even as she watched, the pain of their words lingered in her mind. The harshness of their comments seemed to echo through her thoughts, drowning out the information on the screen. As she ate and cried, her sobs mingled with the documentary's narration, creating a discordant soundtrack to her misery.

Minutes turned into hours, and Amélie's tears showed no signs of stopping. Her face was streaked with mascara and tears, and her hands were covered in ice cream. It felt like she was caught in an emotional storm, unable to escape the waves of hurt that crashed over her.

Just then, there was a gentle knock on her door. Henri, Grand-mère Marie, and Grand-père Alain entered, their expressions filled with concern. They had seen Amélie's distress and came to offer their support.

"Amélie, mon ange," Henri said softly, his voice full of warmth. "Nous avons entendu ce que les autres disaient. Ne les écoute pas."

Grand-mère Marie sat beside Amélie on the bed, placing a comforting hand on her shoulder. "Tu es une personne merveilleuse, Amélie. Ne laisse personne te faire douter de toi-même."

Grand-père Alain, looking more tired but still full of love, added, "We're proud of you. What you did for me was extraordinary, and we want you to know how much you mean to us."

Amélie looked at them, her eyes red and puffy. "I don't understand why they say those things. I was just trying to help."

Henri reached into his pocket and pulled out a small bundle of cash. "We want you to have this, Amélie," he said, holding out 500 euros. "For everything you've done, and for who you are. Please, take it."

Amélie shook her head, her emotions too tangled to form coherent words. "I can't... it's too much. I don't deserve this."

"Don't argue with us, darling," Grand-mère Marie said gently. "It's a token of our appreciation. You've been through so much, and you deserve to know how much we value you."

Grand-père Alain nodded in agreement. "It's not just about what you did for me. It's about who you are and the love you give."

Despite her protests, Amélie could see the sincerity in their eyes. They were determined to offer their support, and their gestures of kindness were a balm to her wounded heart. Reluctantly, she accepted the money, feeling a mixture of gratitude and discomfort.

"Thank you," Amélie whispered, hugging them tightly. "I really appreciate it. I'm sorry for being so upset."

Henri smiled gently. "There's no need to apologize. We all have our moments. What matters is that we're here for each other."

With their support bolstering her spirits, Amélie felt a renewed sense of strength. The emotional turmoil of the past few days seemed to lift, if only slightly, as she realized she was surrounded by people who truly cared for her.

Soon, it was time to leave for Nice. The family gathered their belongings and prepared for the journey. Amélie took one last look around the house, the place that had been both a source of comfort and a battleground of emotions. She felt a pang of sadness as she said goodbye to Grand-père Alain, Grand-mère Marie, and Henri.

"We'll see you soon," Henri said warmly, shaking Amélie's hand. "Take care of yourselves, and remember, you're always in our hearts."

As they drove away from the Dubois estate, Amélie looked out the window, watching the familiar landmarks of Paris recede in the distance. She was grateful for the love and support of her family and determined to return to Nice with a renewed sense of hope and resilience.

The road ahead was long, but with her family by her side, Amélie felt ready to face whatever challenges lay ahead. She knew that no matter where life took her, she had the strength and support to navigate the ups and downs, and she was determined to make the most of every moment.

Amélie's Diary

Dear Diary,

Today was a whirlwind of emotions. The day started with a mix of relief and sadness as we prepared to return to Nice. Even though we were heading back home, the events of the past few days weighed heavily on me.

Grand-père Alain was recovering well, and it was comforting to see him back home. His gratitude and the support from Henri and Grand-mère Marie were heartwarming. They gave me money as a token of appreciation for what I did, but it felt awkward accepting it. They were insistent, though, and their kindness was touching.

I felt overwhelmed by everything that had happened. The words of criticism from Alex, James, Lèon, and Èlodie had stung deeply. I overheard them talking badly about me, and it hurt so much. Their harsh comments made me feel like I was alone in my struggles and achievements.

To cope, I retreated to my room, watched a medical documentary, and ate ice cream. It was a small comfort but didn't quite erase the pain. I cried a lot, trying to process everything. Despite the comfort from Henri, Grand-mère Marie, and Grand-père Alain, I couldn't shake the feeling of hurt and sadness.

Eventually, we had to leave for Nice. As we boarded the flight, I was filled with a mix of relief and melancholy. It's hard to leave behind the warmth of family, but I know that I'll carry their support and love with me.

Today taught me about the complexities of family, emotions, and the strength required to face challenges. I'm grateful for the support I received, but it's clear that the road ahead will have its own set of challenges.

Goodnight, Diary. I'm hoping for a better tomorrow.

Love,

Amélie

Chapter 6: Reunion with Friends

The drive from Paris to Nice was long, but the anticipation of returning home made it somewhat bearable. Amélie spent most of the journey gazing out the window, lost in thought. The recent events weighed heavily on her mind, but the thought of reuniting with her friends brought a glimmer of excitement amidst her lingering sadness.

As the family pulled into their driveway, the familiar sight of their house was both comforting and reassuring. Amélie quickly spotted Philippe and Cécile DuPont, who had been waiting eagerly for their arrival. The DuPont twins were among her closest friends, and seeing them after the stressful events of the past week was a welcome relief.

Philippe and Cécile were standing outside, waving enthusiastically as the car approached. Philippe, always the more outgoing of the two, was bouncing with excitement, while Cécile, with her more reserved nature, had a broad smile on her face. The moment Amélie and Alex stepped out of the car, the twins rushed forward to greet them.

"Amélie! Alex! We've missed you so much!" Philippe exclaimed, enveloping them both in a big hug.

"Welcome back!" Cécile added, her eyes shining with joy. "We've been looking forward to seeing you."

Amélie felt a wave of relief wash over her as she hugged her friends. It was comforting to be surrounded by familiar faces, especially after the emotional upheaval she had been through. Philippe and Cécile's warmth and enthusiasm provided a much-needed distraction from the recent stresses.

"We missed you guys too," Amélie said, her voice a little shaky but genuine. "It's been a crazy few days."

Philippe and Cécile led them inside, where a small welcome-home party had been set up. There were balloons, banners, and a spread of snacks and treats. The house felt lively and filled with the kind of joy that was a stark contrast to the somber mood of the past week.

As they settled in, Philippe and Cécile excitedly filled Amélie and Alex in on what they had missed while they were away. "We've had so much fun," Philippe said, recounting a recent school event. "And we've been practicing for our next football match. You've got to come and watch!"

Cécile chimed in, "And I've been working on a new art project that I'd love to show you. I think you'll like it!"

The conversation flowed easily, and Amélie felt the heaviness in her heart begin to lift. Being with her friends reminded her of the simple joys of life and provided a welcome escape from her worries. They talked about everything from school to their plans for the upcoming holidays, and it felt like a small piece of normalcy had returned to her life.

During a quieter moment, Amélie pulled Philippe and Cécile aside. "Can I talk to you guys for a minute?" she asked, her voice barely above a whisper.

"Of course," Cécile replied, sensing that something was troubling her friend.

The three of them sat in a quiet corner of the room. Amélie took a deep breath before speaking. "I've been having a really hard time lately. Things with Grand-père Alain, and then overhearing some of the things people said about me—it's been a lot to handle."

Philippe and Cécile listened intently, their expressions filled with concern. Philippe placed a comforting hand on Amélie's shoulder. "I'm so sorry you've been going through this. We're here for you, no matter what."

Cécile nodded in agreement. "Yes, absolutely. You're one of our closest friends, and we want to support you however we can. If you need to talk, we're always here."

Amélie felt a wave of gratitude. Having friends who understood and cared made all the difference. "Thank you," she said, her voice breaking slightly. "It means a lot to know that I have you both."

As the evening continued, the mood lightened, and the party went on with laughter and games. Philippe and Cécile made sure that Amélie and Alex felt included and entertained, and it was clear that their friendship was a source of great comfort.

When the time came to say goodbye, Amélie hugged her friends tightly. "Thanks for being such great friends. I really needed this today."

Philippe and Cécile smiled warmly. "We're always here for you," Philippe said. "Don't hesitate to reach out if you need anything."

As Amélie and Alex walked back to their house, Amélie felt a renewed sense of hope. The support from her friends, combined with the love and care of her family, was helping her navigate through the difficult times. The challenges ahead seemed a little less daunting with the strength of her friendships and the support of those who cared about her.

The day ended on a hopeful note, with Amélie feeling more positive about the future. Her friends' unwavering support had provided a much-needed boost to her spirits, reminding her of the value of true friendship and the importance of having people who genuinely care.

And so, as she settled into her bed that night, Amélie felt a sense of peace, knowing that she was surrounded by love and support, ready to face whatever came next with renewed strength and optimism.

Amélie's Diary

Dear Diary,

Today has been a bit of a rollercoaster. After yesterday's warm reunion with Philippe and Cécile, I hoped that things would start to feel more normal. But the day brought its own set of challenges.

This morning, I woke up feeling more refreshed than I had in a while. The comforting presence of my friends and the peaceful night's sleep had helped lift my spirits. I decided to spend some time catching up on my medical journals. Les nouveaux journaux que j'ai reçus de l'oncle Henri et de grand-mère Marie sont incroyables. Ils sont pleins de nouvelles informations et de techniques que j'ai hâte d'apprendre.

However, as I was engrossed in reading, I overheard some conversations that made me feel uneasy. I was trying to avoid thinking about the previous tensions and focusing on my studies, but it seems I couldn't fully escape the uncomfortable atmosphere. I tried to brush it off, but it stung a little.

Cécile and Philippe came over to visit, and they could tell something was off. I tried to put on a brave face and act like everything was fine, but they could see through me. During our catch-up, I found myself opening up about how I was feeling. It felt good to share, and their support was incredibly comforting. Philippe and Cécile both reassured me that they were there for me and that their friendship meant a lot.

In the afternoon, we decided to do something fun to take my mind off things. Philippe suggested we go for a walk in the park, and it was a great idea. Le temps était magnifique—le soleil brillait et l'air était frais. We walked around, talked, and laughed. Cécile showed me some of her recent art sketches, and Philippe talked about his latest football match. The distraction was exactly what I needed.

Later, when we returned home, I felt a bit more at ease. I spent the evening preparing a new recipe I had been excited to try. I wanted to do something nice for the family after the past few days of tension. I decided to make a special dessert, a gâteau au chocolat, which I thought would be a nice treat.

As I was baking, I found myself reflecting on everything that had happened recently. Les difficultés que j'ai rencontrées m'ont appris beaucoup sur moi-même et sur les gens autour de moi. I realized that although there are challenges and misunderstandings, there are also moments of joy and support that help balance things out.

During dinner, I served the gâteau au chocolat. It was met with smiles and compliments, which made me feel better. I was glad to see everyone enjoying it and appreciating my effort.

Before bed, I took some time to write in you, Diary. I find that putting my thoughts into words helps me process everything. Aujourd'hui a été difficile, mais il y a eu des moments de réconfort et de joie. I'm learning to navigate the complexities of emotions and relationships, and I'm grateful for the support of those who truly care about me.

I hope that as time goes on, things will settle down and I'll find a better balance. For now, I'm trying to focus on the positives and take things one day at a time.

Goodnight, Diary. Thank you for listening and for being my companion.

With love,

Amélie

Chapter 7: A Disturbing Revelation

The days following their return to Nice were filled with a mix of routine and quiet reflection for Amélie and her family. The recent visit to Paris had left its mark, but the comfort of home and the presence of their friends Philippe and Cécile brought some semblance of normalcy back into their lives.

It was a bright Sunday morning when François suggested they have a video call with Grand-père Alain and Grand-mère Marie. "It's been a while since we talked to them," he said, looking at Isabelle. "And it would be good to catch up after everything that happened in Paris."

Amélie agreed. Despite the recent tension, she missed her grandparents dearly. They had always been a source of wisdom and love, and she was eager to see their faces and hear their voices.

The family gathered in the living room, where François set up the laptop on the coffee table. The screen flickered to life, and within moments, the familiar faces of Marie and Alain appeared. Grand-mère Marie was beaming, her warm smile filling the screen.

"Bonjour, mes chers!" she greeted, her voice full of joy. "It's so good to see you all!"

"Bonjour, Grand-mère! Bonjour, Grand-père!" Amélie and Alex chimed in together.

"Hello, everyone," Alain said, his voice slightly strained but cheerful. "How are you all doing back in Nice?"

As they began to chat, Amélie couldn't help but notice that Alain looked more tired than usual. His face seemed paler, and there was a slight tremor in his hands. He was smiling and participating in the conversation, but something about his demeanour seemed off.

Marie talked about the weather in Paris, the books she had been reading, and the garden she was tending to. Alain added a few comments here and there, but mostly listened. Amélie kept a close eye on him, growing more concerned by the minute.

"How have you been feeling, Grand-père?" Amélie finally asked, unable to hide the worry in her voice.

Alain glanced at her and then at Marie. "Oh, I've been fine, Amélie," he replied, attempting to sound reassuring. "Just the usual old age aches and pains."

But Amélie wasn't convinced. Something was clearly not right. She exchanged a worried glance with her parents, who also seemed to notice Alain's condition.

"Are you sure, Papa?" François asked gently. "You look a bit tired."

Marie sighed, her smile fading slightly. "He's been having some health issues lately, but he's stubborn and won't admit it," she said, her tone a mix of affection and exasperation.

Alain tried to wave off the concern. "It's nothing to worry about. Just a bit of fatigue."

But as the conversation continued, Alain's symptoms became more apparent. He seemed short of breath and had to pause frequently to catch it. At one point, he even clutched his chest slightly, trying to hide the discomfort.

Amélie's heart sank. She knew the signs all too well. She had read about them in her medical journals and seen them in the hospital during her visits. Alain was showing symptoms of late-stage heart disease, and it was serious.

"Grand-père, please," she said, her voice trembling. "You need to see a doctor. This isn't just fatigue."

Alain looked at her, his eyes filled with a mix of love and resignation. "I know, ma petite. I promise I'll go for a check-up."

François and Isabelle both nodded in agreement. "We'll make sure of it," François said firmly. "Your health is too important to ignore."

The rest of the call was filled with reassurances and promises to take care of Alain's health. Amélie felt a knot of worry settle in her stomach, but she tried to remain hopeful. She knew that early detection and treatment could make a big difference.

As they said their goodbyes and ended the call, Amélie felt a wave of emotions crash over her. She was scared for her grandfather but also determined to help in any way she could. She looked at her parents, who shared her concern.

"We need to keep an eye on him," Isabelle said softly. "Make sure he gets the medical attention he needs."

Amélie nodded. "I'll do some research and see if I can find any specialists who might be able to help."

François placed a comforting hand on her shoulder. "We'll get through this together, Amélie. Your Grand-père is strong, and we'll do everything we can to support him."

Later that evening, Amélie found herself alone in her room, reflecting on the day's events. She pulled out her medical journals and began to read about heart disease, looking for any information that might help. She was determined to stay informed and be ready to assist in any way possible.

As she read, she couldn't help but feel a sense of helplessness. Despite all her knowledge and passion for medicine, she was still just a young girl, and the reality of her grandfather's condition was overwhelming.

But she also felt a spark of determination. Her love for her family and her desire to become a doctor fuelled her resolve. She would do everything in her power to help Alain and make sure he received the best care possible.

"Je t'aime, Grand-père," she whispered to herself, feeling a tear roll down her cheek. "I'll do everything I can to help you."

With that promise in her heart, Amélie continued to study late into the night, driven by her love for her family and her dream of one day becoming a doctor who could make a difference in the lives of those she loved.

Amélie's Diary

Dear Diary,

Today was one of the most emotionally taxing days I've ever experienced. It started out so normal, and yet it ended in a way that has left me shaken to my core.

This morning, Papa suggested we have a video call with Grand-père Alain and Grand-mère Marie. I was thrilled at the idea, especially after the recent trip to Paris. It felt like it had been ages since we saw them, even though it was only a few days ago. Seeing their faces on the screen always brings a sense of warmth and comfort, like a cozy blanket on a cold day.

When the call connected and their familiar faces filled the screen, I felt an immediate rush of happiness. Grand-mère Marie was as lively and cheerful as always, but Grand-père Alain... he didn't look quite right. He seemed tired, and there was a shadow of something more serious behind his eyes.

As we chatted, I tried to focus on the conversation, but I couldn't stop watching him. J'étais tellement inquiète. He seemed out of breath, and there were moments when he clutched his chest slightly, thinking no one noticed. I noticed. We all did.

At first, I tried to push down the fear. Maybe it was just my imagination running wild. But as the call went on, it became clear that something was very wrong. When I finally gathered the courage to ask how he was feeling, his attempt to reassure me fell flat. Even Grand-mère Marie couldn't hide her concern.

"Il a eu quelques problèmes de santé récemment, mais il ne veut pas l'admettre," she said, her voice a mix of love and frustration. Hearing this, I felt my heart sink even further.

I knew the signs. I had seen them in my medical journals, in the hospital, in the eyes of patients struggling with serious conditions. Alain was showing symptoms of late-stage heart disease.

The rest of the conversation was a blur of promises and reassurances. Grand-père Alain agreed to see a doctor, but I could see the resignation in his eyes. He was trying to be strong for us, but I knew how scared he must be.

When the call ended, I felt a wave of emotions crash over me. J'avais tellement peur pour lui. My mind kept racing with worst-case scenarios, and I felt helpless. Despite all my studies and my dreams of becoming a doctor, I was just a young girl facing the terrifying reality of possibly losing someone I love dearly.

Mama, Papa, and Alex tried to comfort me, promising that we would make sure Grand-père gets the best care. But the knot in my stomach wouldn't go away. I felt a burning need to do something, anything, to help.

I spent the rest of the evening diving into my medical journals, looking up everything I could about heart disease and treatments. I was determined to find information that could help, even if it was just a small piece of the puzzle. Je voulais tellement l'aider.

Yet, as I read, the sense of helplessness grew. Knowledge is power, they say, but knowing so much about his condition made the situation feel even more dire. The thought of losing Grand-père was unbearable.

Still, there was a spark of determination within me. My love for my family and my desire to help others fuelled my resolve. I knew I couldn't fix everything, but I could stay informed, be there for him, and support him however I could.

"Je t'aime, Grand-père," I whispered as I closed my journals for the night. "I'll do everything I can to help you."

I went to bed with a heavy heart, but also with a renewed sense of purpose. This was a test of my strength, my knowledge, and my love. And I would face it head-on, just like I promised Grand-père.

Thank you for listening, Diary. Writing everything down helps me make sense of it all, and somehow, it feels like I'm sharing the burden with you.

Goodnight.
Avec amour,
Amélie

Chapter 8: A Day of Worry

The morning air was crisp, and the sun peeked over the horizon, casting a gentle glow on the Dubois household. Despite the bright start, a heavy sense of unease lingered in the air. Amélie woke up with a tight knot in her stomach, a premonition that something was not right. She quickly got dressed and joined her family for breakfast, trying to shake off the feeling.

François and Isabelle exchanged worried glances over their coffee cups. They had received a phone call early that morning from Grand-mère Marie, informing them that Alain had been admitted to the hospital. His condition had worsened overnight, and it was clear he needed immediate medical attention.

"Amélie, we need to talk," François said gently, pulling his daughter aside. "Grand-père Alain is in the hospital. He wasn't feeling well, and they decided it was best to admit him for further tests and observation."

Amélie's heart dropped. "Is he going to be okay?" she asked, her voice trembling.

"We don't know yet, ma chérie. The doctors are doing everything they can," Isabelle said, trying to offer some comfort. "But for now, you need to go to school. We'll keep you updated throughout the day."

It was the last thing Amélie wanted to hear. The thought of sitting in a classroom, going through the motions of a regular school day while her grandfather was in the hospital, felt unbearable. But she knew her parents were right. She had to go to school and try to focus.

As she walked to school with Alex, her mind was in a fog. Alex tried to cheer her up, talking about their plans for the weekend and the latest football match he'd watched, but Amélie could barely muster a smile. Her thoughts were consumed by images of Grand-père Alain in a hospital bed, surrounded by doctors and nurses.

The school day dragged on, each minute feeling like an eternity. Amélie tried to concentrate on her lessons, but her mind kept drifting back to her grandfather. She kept checking her phone, hoping for any news from her parents. The constant worry gnawed at her, making it hard to focus on anything else.

During lunch, she sat with Philippe and Cécile, who immediately noticed something was wrong. "Amélie, tu vas bien?" Philippe asked, his brow furrowed with concern.

"Non, pas vraiment," she admitted. "Grand-père Alain est à l'hôpital. Je suis tellement inquiète pour lui."

Cécile reached out and squeezed her hand. "Nous sommes là pour toi, Amélie. Si tu as besoin de parler ou de quoi que ce soit, dis-le-nous."

"Merci," Amélie said, grateful for their support. "C'est juste... tellement difficile de ne pas être là avec lui."

The rest of the afternoon was a blur. Amélie went through the motions of her classes, but her heart wasn't in it. She kept imagining the worst-case scenarios, her anxiety growing with each passing hour. By the time the final bell rang, she felt utterly drained.

As soon as she got home, she dropped her bag by the door and rushed to find her parents. Isabelle was in the kitchen, her phone in hand, and François was pacing the living room.

"Maman, Papa, avez-vous des nouvelles?" Amélie asked, her voice shaking.

Isabelle looked up, her expression a mix of relief and worry. "Yes, we have news. Grand-père Alain is stable for now, but he needs to stay in the hospital for more tests. They're worried about his heart."

Tears welled up in Amélie's eyes. "Je veux aller le voir," she said, her voice breaking.

"I know, ma chérie," François said, wrapping his arms around her. "But right now, it's best if we give him some time to rest and let the doctors do their work. We'll visit him as soon as we can."

Amélie nodded, though the ache in her chest didn't lessen. She spent the rest of the evening trying to distract herself with homework and chores, but her mind kept drifting back to her grandfather.

Later that night, as she lay in bed, Amélie couldn't hold back her tears any longer. She buried her face in her pillow and sobbed, the worry and fear overwhelming her. She felt so helpless, so far away from the person she loved so much.

"Je t'aime, Grand-père," she whispered into the darkness. "Please be okay."

Eventually, exhaustion took over, and she fell into a restless sleep, her dreams filled with images of hospital rooms and doctors' faces. As much as she tried to stay strong, the uncertainty and fear were almost too much to bear.

The next morning, Amélie woke up with puffy eyes and a heavy heart. She had to face another day of school, another day of waiting for news. But she knew she had to keep going, for her grandfather, for her family, and for herself. She would find a way to get through this, one day at a time.

Amélie's Diary

Dear Diary,

Aujourd'hui a été une montagne russe d'émotions. C'est tellement difficile de gérer tout ce qui se passe avec Grand-père Alain à l'hôpital. Every moment feels like a struggle between hope and fear. I feel like my heart is constantly in my throat, waiting for any bit of news, good or bad.

This morning started like any other, but the weight of the situation was ever-present. J'ai essayé de me concentrer sur mes cours, mais c'était presque impossible. My mind kept wandering back to Grand-père Alain. How is he doing? What are the doctors saying? Is he comfortable? Est-ce qu'il pense à nous autant que nous pensons à lui?

I felt like a ghost, floating through the school day without really being present. My friends noticed, of course. Philippe and Cécile tried their best to cheer me up, but their efforts felt like distant echoes. I appreciated their kindness, but nothing could truly lift the cloud hanging over me.

During lunch, I found a quiet corner in the library and tried to distract myself with a medical journal. Reading about the very heart conditions that Grand-père is facing felt surreal. C'était comme si les mots sur la page étaient trop proches de la réalité. I wanted to understand everything, to be prepared for any possible outcome, but it was overwhelming. The more I read, the more frightened I became.

Philippe found me and sat beside me quietly, offering his presence without words. It was comforting in a way, knowing that someone was there, understanding my silence. Cécile joined us a bit later, and we just sat there, a small bubble of solace amidst the storm of my thoughts.

After school, I rushed home, hoping for some news. Maman était au téléphone avec l'hôpital, et Papa avait l'air épuisé. When she hung up, she gave us an update. Grand-père Alain is stable, but they're still running tests. They're worried about his heart and are considering some procedures to help him.

The relief of knowing he was stable was momentary. La peur de ce qui pourrait arriver ensuite est toujours là. I wanted to go to the hospital, to be by his side, to tell him how much I love him, but I knew it wasn't possible. The doctors needed their space to work, and I had to be patient.

Patience. That's what everyone keeps telling me. But it's so hard. Chaque minute passée sans nouvelles semble une éternité. I spent the evening trying to study, but the words blurred together. I found myself staring at my textbooks, unable to absorb anything. The only thing that seemed to help, even a little, was cooking.

Cooking has always been my escape, my way to process my emotions. Ce soir, j'ai décidé de faire du riz frit et du pain sans levain, using the recipes Grand-père loves. It was my way of feeling connected to him, even if he was miles away. As I cooked, I thought about the times we spent together in the kitchen, his gentle guidance, his patient explanations. It brought a bittersweet smile to my face.

When dinner was ready, I set the table and we all sat down to eat. The food brought a sense of normalcy, a brief respite from the constant worry. We talked about our day, shared stories, and tried to keep the conversation light. But beneath it all, we were all thinking the same thing.

After dinner, I retreated to my room. J'ai allumé mon ordinateur et j'ai commencé à regarder un documentaire médical. It was a way to keep my mind occupied, to feel like I was doing something productive. But even as I watched, my thoughts kept drifting back to Grand-père. Would he be proud of me, seeing how much I'm trying to learn and prepare for my future as a doctor?

As the documentary played, I couldn't help but feel the weight of it all. The fear, the uncertainty, the helplessness. It all came crashing down. I reached for the tub of ice cream I'd hidden away, seeking comfort in its sweetness. Je sais que ce n'est pas la meilleure façon de gérer mes émotions, mais en ce moment, c'est tout ce que j'ai.

I ate in silence, tears streaming down my face. The coldness of the ice cream contrasted sharply with the warmth of my tears. I felt so alone, even though I knew my family and friends were there for me. C'est difficile de partager cette douleur, cette peur. It's something I have to work through on my own, in my own way.

Eventually, I fell asleep, exhausted from the day's emotional toll. As I drifted off, I whispered a silent prayer for Grand-père Alain, hoping with all my heart that he would be okay.

Thank you for listening, Diary. Writing it all down helps, even if just a little. Bonne nuit.

Avec amour,

Amélie

Chapter 9: A Long Journey

The morning of January 27th dawned grey and overcast, mirroring the somber mood of the Dubois household. Amélie awoke with a sinking feeling in her stomach, knowing that today would be a long and emotionally draining day. Her grandfather, Alain, had undergone surgery the previous day, and the family had decided it was crucial to be by his side as he recovered. To that end, they would be flying to Canada to be with him and Grand-mère Marie.

Amélie got out of bed and dressed quickly, her mind preoccupied with thoughts of the upcoming journey. The airport was bustling with travelers, and the reality of the trip weighed heavily on her. She joined her family in the kitchen, where the mood was subdued. François and Isabelle were busy with last-minute preparations, while Alex sat at the table, his gaze fixed on his phone.

"Bon matin, ma chérie," Isabelle said softly, handing Amélie a cup of coffee. "Are you ready for the trip?"

"Je suppose," Amélie replied, her voice tinged with apprehension. "I'm worried about Grand-père. How will he be when we get there?"

François placed a reassuring hand on her shoulder. "The doctors are doing everything they can. We need to stay positive and be there for him and for Marie."

They finished breakfast quickly and packed the last of their things. The journey to the airport was quiet, each of them lost in their thoughts. Amélie glanced out the window, watching the familiar scenery of Nice give way to the airport's busy surroundings.

Upon arrival at the airport, the family went through the check-in process and headed to their gate. The anticipation was palpable, and Amélie found herself struggling to focus on anything other than the looming flight. The thought of seeing Grand-père Alain and Grand-mère Marie again provided some comfort, but it was overshadowed by the worry for Alain's health.

As they boarded the plane, Amélie settled into her seat, trying to distract herself with a book. The flight was long and tedious. Every hour seemed to stretch into eternity. The turbulence during the flight only heightened her anxiety, and she found herself repeatedly checking the time, eager to reach their destination.

After what felt like an age, the plane finally touched down in Canada. Amélie, François, Isabelle, and Alex collected their luggage and made their way through the airport. The cold air of Canada hit them as they stepped outside, a sharp contrast to the milder climate they had left behind.

Grand-père Alain and Grand-mère Marie's house was a short drive from the airport. The familiarity of the place brought a bittersweet sense of comfort. Amélie's heart ached at the thought of her grandfather being in the hospital, but she felt a glimmer of hope as they approached the house.

Marie greeted them at the door with tears in her eyes. "Welcome, everyone. I'm so glad you're here."

"Thank you, Marie," François said, embracing her. "We wouldn't have missed this for anything."

Isabelle and Marie quickly caught up, exchanging news and discussing Alain's condition. Meanwhile, Amélie and Alex sat quietly, the weight of the situation hanging heavily on their shoulders.

Later that day, they made their way to the hospital in Québec where Alain was being treated. The drive was filled with a tense silence, broken only by the occasional attempt at conversation. Amélie could feel her heart racing as they arrived at the hospital. The sight of the imposing building only intensified her anxiety.

Upon entering the hospital, they were directed to the waiting area. Amélie's heart pounded as they settled in, the reality of the situation sinking in. She glanced around, taking in the sterile environment of the hospital. It felt so different from the warmth of her grandparents' home.

François approached the reception desk to inquire about Alain's condition. After a brief conversation, he returned to the waiting area with a solemn expression. "The doctors are still monitoring him closely. We'll have to wait a bit longer before we can see him."

Amélie felt a pang of frustration. The waiting was becoming unbearable. She found a quiet corner and tried to collect her thoughts. Her emotions were a turbulent mix of fear, sadness, and helplessness.

The minutes ticked by slowly. Amélie watched the clock, each passing second feeling like an eternity. She was grateful for the presence of her family, but the uncertainty of the situation made it hard to find solace.

Finally, a nurse came to get them. "You can see Mr. Dubois now," she said with a reassuring smile. "He's in stable condition, but he's still resting from the procedure."

Amélie's heart leapt as they followed the nurse to Alain's room. The sight of her grandfather lying in the hospital bed was both a relief and a source of anguish. He looked frail but was surrounded by medical equipment, his breathing steady.

"Grand-père," Amélie said softly, taking his hand in hers. "Nous sommes ici pour toi."

Alain opened his eyes slowly and managed a weak smile. "Amélie, ma petite. C'est un soulagement de vous voir ici."

"I'm so glad we're here," Amélie said, her voice trembling. "How are you feeling?"

"Je me sens mieux, merci. Les médecins disent que je vais m'améliorer," Alain replied. "Mais je suis épuisé."

The family spent time with Alain, talking softly and offering words of encouragement. The atmosphere in the room was filled with a mix of hope and concern. Amélie was grateful for the chance to be with her grandfather, but her worry remained.

As visiting hours drew to a close, the family reluctantly said their goodbyes. Amélie hugged Alain tightly, her heart aching at the sight of him in such a vulnerable state.

"Je reviendrai demain, Grand-père," she promised. "Nous allons tout faire pour que tu te rétablisses rapidement."

"Merci, ma petite," Alain said, his voice filled with emotion. "Votre présence me donne de la force."

Returning to Marie's house, the family gathered for a quiet dinner. The meal was subdued, the conversation focused on Alain's condition and plans for the following days. Amélie found it difficult to eat, her mind preoccupied with thoughts of her grandfather.

After dinner, Amélie retreated to her room. She pulled out her journal and began writing, trying to process the whirlwind of emotions she was experiencing. The entries were a mix of anxiety, hope, and a deep sense of gratitude for the support of her family.

As she prepared for bed, Amélie reflected on the day's events. The journey had been long and emotionally taxing, but being with her family and having the chance to see her grandfather gave her some comfort. She knew there would be more challenges ahead, but for now, she focused on the hope that Alain would continue to improve.

With a heavy heart but a glimmer of hope, Amélie closed her journal and turned off the light. She settled into bed, determined to face the days ahead with strength and resilience.

Amélie's Diary

Dear Diary,

Aujourd'hui a été un jour plein d'émotions. After our long journey to Canada, I had hoped for some relief, but the day brought new challenges.

The morning began with a slight glimmer of hope. We woke up early to visit Grand-père Alain at the hospital. The sunrise over Québec was beautiful, though it didn't quite reach my heart, which remained heavy with worry. I tried to focus on the positive news we had received: the doctors were optimistic about his recovery. Yet, seeing him in such a state was incredibly difficult.

I remember feeling a tight knot in my stomach as we approached his room. Les infirmières nous ont accueillis avec des sourires rassurants. I tried to stay composed, but as soon as I saw Grand-père lying in that hospital bed, I felt tears welling up. I could barely hold back my emotions. He looked so fragile, and I was terrified.

Despite this, I stayed hopeful and tried to be strong for him. "Grand-père, je suis tellement heureuse d'être ici avec toi," I said, trying to sound as reassuring as possible. His eyes lit up when he saw us, and he managed to give a weak smile. "Je suis content de vous voir," he replied, though his voice was barely a whisper.

We spent the morning with him, talking softly and sharing stories to lift his spirits. I brought some of my favourite books and read to him, hoping it would help him relax. François, Isabelle, and Alex did their best to keep the conversation light and positive. Grand-mère Marie joined us, and though she tried to appear strong, I could see the worry etched on her face.

After our visit, we returned to Marie's house. The atmosphere was subdued, and the house felt strangely quiet. Marie tried to prepare a meal for us, but the usual warmth of her cooking was overshadowed by the stress and fatigue we were all feeling. I found it hard to eat. The food was good, but my mind kept drifting back to Grand-père and how he was doing.

Later in the afternoon, we decided to take a brief walk around the neighbourhood. The crisp air was a welcome distraction, and I found some solace in the peaceful surroundings. Walking through the snowy streets of Québec, I tried to clear my mind, but the worry for Grand-père lingered.

In the evening, we returned to the hospital for another visit. This time, I felt a little more composed, but the sight of Grand-père in the hospital bed still brought a pang of sadness. I was grateful for the chance to see him, but each visit seemed to take a toll on my emotions. I tried to focus on keeping our conversations positive and hopeful, though it was challenging.

Before we left the hospital, I took a moment to sit by his bedside. "Je reviendrai demain, Grand-père. Nous allons tout faire pour que tu te rétablisses rapidement," I promised. He squeezed my hand and nodded, a gesture that gave me a small measure of comfort.

Returning to Marie's house, I felt an overwhelming sense of exhaustion. I sat quietly in my room, reflecting on the day. It's hard to put into words how I'm feeling. There's a mixture of fear, hope, and fatigue. I'm trying to stay strong for my family and for Grand-père, but it's not always easy.

Je suis inquiète pour lui, I wrote, feeling the weight of my emotions. I wish I could do more to help him.

Before heading to bed, I tried to write in my journal to process everything that had happened. Writing helps me sort through my feelings, and tonight was no exception. I felt a bit better after pouring my thoughts onto the page, but the worry for Grand-père remains.

J'espère que demain apportera de bonnes nouvelles.

Goodnight, Diary. Here's hoping for a better day tomorrow.

Amélie

Chapter 10: Alain's Last Wish

The morning of January 28th in Quebec began with a heavy, oppressive grey sky, reflecting the solemn mood that enveloped the Dubois family. The cold, biting air seemed to mirror the deep sadness that had settled in their hearts as they made their way to the hospital. The snow-covered landscape outside offered a stark contrast to the intense emotional turmoil within.

Amélie, François, and Isabelle arrived at the hospital early, their faces etched with exhaustion and apprehension. François and Isabelle moved with a quiet determination, their concern for Alain palpable. Amélie, too, felt the crushing weight of the day ahead, her heart heavy with the realization that this might be her grandfather's final moments.

The family was led to a small waiting room, the sterile environment offering little comfort. The ticking of the clock on the wall seemed to magnify the tension, each minute stretching into what felt like an eternity. The steady beeping of medical equipment in the background was a constant reminder of the fragility of the situation.

After what felt like an eternity, a doctor arrived with a grave expression. "Mr. Dubois's condition has significantly worsened," he announced. "The surgery was only a temporary measure, and despite our best efforts, he's now in the final stages of his illness. It's crucial that you prepare yourselves for the inevitable."

The doctor's words were a heavy blow to the family. François and Isabelle exchanged pained glances, their faces reflecting the weight of the news. Amélie felt a lump form in her throat as the reality of the situation hit her. The severity of Alain's condition was becoming all too clear.

The family was escorted to Alain's room. The sight that greeted them was heart-wrenching. Alain, once a robust and lively figure, now lay in the hospital bed looking frail and diminished. The room was dimly lit, filled with the hum of medical machines and the rhythmic beeping of the heart monitor.

Amélie approached the bedside with a heavy heart. She reached out to hold Alain's hand, its frailty a stark contrast to her own. Tears filled her eyes as she struggled to find the right words. "Grand-père," she whispered, her voice trembling. "I'm so sorry. I wish there was more I could do."

François and Isabelle took their turns speaking to Alain, their voices choked with emotion. They expressed their love, regrets, and hopes, their words a mixture of comfort and farewell. Amélie stood by, feeling her heart break with every word shared.

Marie, Alain's devoted wife, arrived soon after. Her face was etched with grief as she took Alain's hand in hers, her fingers trembling. "Alain, mon amour," she said softly. "Nous avons partagé tant de belles années ensemble. Je suis tellement fière de toi. Nous allons toujours t'aimer."

The room was filled with the soft sounds of sobbing and whispered words of love. Each family member took their turn at Alain's bedside, their voices heavy with emotion. Amélie held onto her grandfather's hand, trying to convey all the love and gratitude she felt.

As time passed, Alain's condition continued to decline. The beeping of the heart monitor grew increasingly erratic, and the medical staff worked tirelessly to stabilize him. Despite their efforts, it was evident that Alain was nearing the end. The atmosphere in the room grew heavier with each passing moment.

Amélie watched with a heavy heart as the medical staff did everything they could to help Alain. The beeping of the heart monitor became more erratic, reflecting the fragility of Alain's condition. The room was filled with a profound sense of sadness, punctuated only by the soft sounds of family members offering their final goodbyes.

Alain's breathing grew more labored, and his once-strong frame seemed to weaken further with each minute. The family gathered close, their hands reaching out to touch him, offering their final goodbyes.

The beeping of the heart monitor became increasingly irregular, mirroring the decline in Alain's condition.

With great effort, Alain managed to speak his final words. His voice was a faint whisper, but his words were clear and resonant. He looked at each family member in turn, his eyes filled with love and pride. "I love you and will forever be in your hearts," he said softly as he took his last breath.

Amélie's Diary

Today was unimaginably hard. The morning was cold and grey, reflecting the heaviness in my heart. The snow-covered streets of Quebec seemed so distant from the warmth of Paris and Nice, mirroring my own sense of disconnect.

The drive to the hospital was silent, filled with tension. François and Isabelle were quiet, their worry palpable. I sat in the back, staring out at the snow, feeling a profound helplessness. The snow seemed to cover everything in a white veil, as if trying to hide the harsh reality we were facing.

Quand nous sommes arrivés à l'hôpital, l'atmosphère était lourde. Nous avons été dirigés vers la salle d'attente, où le silence était pesant, seulement interrompu par le bourdonnement des machines et les pas des médecins. Chaque minute semblait interminable.

When the doctor came to speak with us, his grave expression was like a blow to the stomach. He told us Alain's condition had worsened despite the surgery. We needed to prepare for the worst. The words hit us hard. François and Isabelle's faces crumbled, and I felt a knot tighten in my throat.

We were led to Alain's room, and seeing him there was heartbreaking. The room was dimly lit, filled with the low hum of equipment and the rhythmic beeping of the heart monitor. Alain lay in bed, looking so frail. It was a painful reminder of how quickly things can change.

En entrant dans la chambre, j'ai eu du mal à retenir mes larmes. Alain avait l'air si faible. Je lui ai pris la main, sentant la chaleur s'éteindre lentement. Chaque minute était une torture, et je me sentais complètement impuissante.

François and Isabelle spoke to Alain with such tenderness, their voices filled with emotion. They told him how much he meant to them, how much they loved him. Watching them, I felt a deep sadness. Every word they spoke felt like a blow to my heart.

When Grand-mère Marie arrived, she held Alain's hand with infinite gentleness. Her face was marked by grief, but she tried to stay strong. Her words were full of affection and sorrow. The room was filled with a heavy, collective sadness.

As time went on, Alain's condition worsened. The heart monitor's beeping became more irregular. Each beep felt more uncertain than the last. The room seemed to close in on us. My heart was pounding, and I felt overwhelmed.

Au fur et à mesure que la condition de Grand-père se détériorait, mon angoisse grandissait. La pièce devenait de plus en plus froide, et chaque seconde semblait durer une éternité. J'avais l'impression de ne pas pouvoir respirer.

When Alain spoke his final words, it was a moment of intense emotion. His voice was weak, but each word was filled with profound love. "I love you and will forever be in your hearts." These words resonated in the room, heavy with meaning. I couldn't hold back my tears as I tried to grasp the significance of his final message.

La pièce est devenue silencieuse après ses derniers mots. Le bruit des machines s'est estompé, laissant place à un calme lourd. Alain est finalement parti, laissant derrière lui une famille dévastée mais unie dans la douleur. Nous nous sommes regroupés autour du lit, cherchant du réconfort les uns dans les autres.

As I try to sleep tonight, his last words keep playing in my mind. They are both a comfort and a painful reminder of his absence. Even in this sorrow, his love feels like a guiding light, a beacon in the darkness. I'm grateful for the moments we shared and for his final message.

Je me souviens de lui avec amour et gratitude, malgré la douleur. Ses derniers mots seront toujours gravés dans mon cœur. Même s'il est parti, son esprit continuera de nous guider.

Grand-père Alain, tu resteras toujours avec nous, dans nos cœurs et nos souvenirs. Votre amour continuera de nous éclairer à travers les moments difficiles.

Avec Amour,

Amélie

Chapter 11: Strength in Sorrow

The following days after Alain's passing were a whirlwind of grief and responsibilities. The Dubois family found themselves navigating the tumultuous waters of sorrow, trying to find a semblance of normalcy while grappling with the profound loss of their beloved patriarch.

Back in Nice, the atmosphere in the Dubois household was palpably sombre. Isabelle and François had returned to work, attempting to bury their grief in their routines. Alex tried to find solace in his football, spending long hours on the field, practicing relentlessly. But for Amélie, the pain was much harder to compartmentalize.

Every morning, she would wake up with a heavy heart, the weight of her grief pressing down on her like a stone. Her usual morning routine—making breakfast for the family, reviewing medical journals, practicing the violin—felt hollow. The joy she once found in these activities seemed to have evaporated, leaving behind a lingering sadness.

One morning, as she sat at the breakfast table, her mind drifting back to the last moments with Alain, François gently placed a hand on her shoulder.

"Amélie," he said softly, "I know it's hard. But we need to find a way to move forward. Alain wouldn't want us to be consumed by our grief."

Amélie nodded, tears welling up in her eyes. "I know, Papa. It's just... it's hard to imagine life without him."

François squeezed her shoulder reassuringly. "He will always be with us, in our hearts and memories. And we have to honour him by living our lives to the fullest, just as he would have wanted."

These words, though comforting, did little to alleviate the ache in Amélie's heart. But she knew her father was right. She needed to find a way to cope, to keep going despite the pain.

She threw herself into her studies, spending hours in her room, reading and taking notes, immersing herself in the world of medicine.

The knowledge she gained became a refuge, a way to distract herself from the overwhelming sadness.

Meanwhile, the rest of the family was dealing with their grief in their own ways. Isabelle, ever the pillar of strength, tried to keep the household running smoothly. She would often be found in the kitchen, preparing meals with a quiet determination, the scent of freshly baked bread or simmering stews filling the house, providing a semblance of comfort.

Alex, though deeply affected by Alain's death, channelled his emotions into his passion for football. His practice sessions became more intense, his focus unwavering. He rarely spoke about his feelings, but Amélie could see the sadness in his eyes, the way he would sometimes stare off into the distance, lost in thought.

In the evenings, the family would gather in the living room, trying to maintain a sense of normalcy. They would watch TV together, play board games, or simply sit and talk. These moments, though tinged with sadness, were also filled with love and support, a reminder that they still had each other.

One night, as they were sitting together, the phone rang. It was Marie, calling from Canada. Her voice was a soothing balm, a connection to the loved one they had lost.

"How are you holding up, my dear ones?" she asked, her voice gentle.

"We're managing, Maman," Isabelle replied. "It's hard, but we're trying to stay strong."

Marie sighed. "I know it's difficult. But remember, Alain would want you to find happiness. He wouldn't want you to be burdened by sorrow."

Amélie, listening to the conversation, felt a tear slip down her cheek. She missed her grandparents terribly, the comfort and wisdom they provided. But she knew Marie was right. They needed to find a way to move forward.

In the weeks that followed, Amélie continued to grapple with her emotions. There were days when the grief felt unbearable, when the sadness threatened to overwhelm her. But she found solace in her studies, in the support of her family, and in the memories of Alain.

One afternoon, as she was going through Alain's old medical journals, she came across a letter he had written to her. It was dated a few months before his death, filled with words of encouragement and love.

Dear Amélie,

I am so proud of the young woman you are becoming. Your passion for medicine, your kindness, and your determination inspire me every day. I know you will achieve great things, and I want you to remember that I will always be with you, cheering you on from afar.

Stay strong, my dear. Life is full of challenges, but you have the strength and resilience to overcome them. Keep pursuing your dreams, and never lose sight of the incredible person you are.

With all my love,

Grand-père Alain

Reading the letter, Amélie felt a renewed sense of purpose. Alain's words were a reminder of the love and support he had always shown her. She realized that she needed to honour his memory by continuing to pursue her dreams, by staying strong in the face of adversity.

She folded the letter carefully, placing it back in the journal. With a deep breath, she wiped away her tears and stood up, feeling a renewed determination.

In the days that followed, she threw herself even more into her studies. She spent long hours in the library, reading medical textbooks, taking detailed notes, and practicing surgical techniques. Her dedication was unwavering, fuelled by the memory of Alain's words.

Her family noticed the change in her. François and Isabelle were proud of her resilience, seeing how she channelled her grief into something positive. Alex, too, admired her strength, though he still found it hard to express his own emotions.

One evening, as they were sitting together in the living room, Alex turned to Amélie.

"I'm proud of you, Amélie," he said, his voice sincere. "I know it's been hard, but you're doing great."

Amélie smiled, feeling a warmth spread through her heart. "Thanks, Alex. It means a lot."

They sat in comfortable silence, the bond between them growing stronger. In their shared grief, they found a deeper connection, a renewed appreciation for each other.

As the weeks turned into months, the pain of Alain's loss began to ease, replaced by a deep sense of gratitude for the time they had spent together. The Dubois family continued to find strength in each other, navigating the ups and downs of life with resilience and love.

For Amélie, the journey was far from over. But with her family by her side and Alain's words guiding her, she knew she could face whatever challenges lay ahead. The path was difficult, but she was determined to keep moving forward, to honour Alain's memory by living a life filled with purpose and love.

Amélie's Diary

Today was an emotional rollercoaster. It's been one of the hardest days I've ever had to endure. I can't believe Grand-père Alain is gone. The reality of it all is so overwhelming. I feel like a part of me has been torn away, leaving an empty space that aches with sorrow.

Quand nous sommes arrivés à l'hôpital, j'ai eu du mal à comprendre ce qui se passait. Seeing Grand-père Alain in that state was heartbreaking. He looked so fragile, so unlike the strong, vibrant man I remember. It was hard to reconcile the image of him lying there with the memories of him teaching me, guiding me, always full of life and energy.

Being surrounded by my family was both comforting and suffocating. I could see the pain in their eyes, the way they tried to stay strong for each other. We all felt the weight of loss, but it was especially hard for me. Grand-père Alain was my mentor, my inspiration. He believed in me when I doubted myself, always encouraging me to pursue my dreams. Losing him feels like losing a part of my own identity.

When he whispered his final words, "I love you and will forever be in your hearts," it felt like a dagger to my heart. Those words were filled with so much love and pain. I will cherish them forever, but they also serve as a reminder of what I've lost. How do I go on from here?

La douleur est si vive, si intense. I keep replaying his last moments over and over in my head, wishing I could have done something more, something to save him. The logical part of me knows there was nothing I could do, but the emotional part of me can't help but feel guilty, as if I should have been able to prevent this somehow.

Maman et Papa ont été incroyables. They have been my rock, supporting me through this, reminding me that it's okay to grieve, to feel the pain. But it's hard to accept their comfort when I feel so lost. It's like I'm in a fog, and everything around me is just a blur. Their words, their hugs—they help, but they don't take away the emptiness.

Alex has been quiet. He throws himself into his football, using it as a distraction, I suppose. I wish I could do the same, find something to take my mind off the pain. But everything I do, everything I see, reminds me of Grand-père Alain. It's like his presence is everywhere, yet he's not here, and that contradiction is tearing me apart.

Today, I tried to study, to lose myself in my books, but it was impossible to focus. Every time I read a sentence, I would see his face, hear his voice, telling me to push on, to never give up. I can't believe he's really gone. How can I continue without his guidance, his support?

Je me sens tellement seule. I know my family is here, and they love me, but this grief is so personal, so isolating. It's like a shadow that follows me, no matter where I go, no matter what I do. I can't escape it, can't outrun it. The sadness is a constant companion, whispering in my ear, reminding me of my loss.

I remember the times we spent together, the lessons he taught me, the stories he shared. Those memories are precious, but they also hurt. It's a bittersweet pain, one that I treasure because it keeps him close, but it also cuts deep, reminding me of what I can never have again.

Il y a des moments où je me demande comment je vais continuer. How do I find the strength to move on, to keep pursuing my dreams without him? He was my anchor, my guide. Now, I feel adrift, lost in a sea of emotions that I don't know how to navigate.

Maman me dit que le temps guérit toutes les blessures, but right now, it feels like this pain will never go away. It's a constant, gnawing ache, one that I don't know how to soothe. I try to be strong, for myself, for my family, but it's so hard.

Je sais qu'il voudrait que je continue, que je poursuive mes rêves. But it feels impossible right now. The world seems so bleak, so empty without him. I try to hold onto his words, his encouragement, but it's difficult when the sadness is so overwhelming.

Being at the hospital today, seeing him for the last time, was one of the hardest things I've ever done. Saying goodbye, knowing I would never see him again, was heartbreaking. I wanted to hold onto him, to keep him with me, but I knew I had to let go. It was the right thing to do, but it hurt so much.

Le soutien de ma famille est précieux. They are trying so hard to help me through this, to be there for me. I can see their pain, too, and it breaks my heart. We are all struggling, trying to cope with this loss, each in our own way. It's a collective grief, but it's also deeply personal.

I think about the future, about how I will navigate it without him. It's a daunting thought, one that fills me with dread. But I know I have to try. For him, for myself, for my family. I have to find a way to move forward, to keep living, even though it feels so hard right now.

Les souvenirs de Grand-père Alain sont précieux. They are a source of comfort, a reminder of the love and wisdom he shared with me. I hold onto them tightly, using them as a beacon in this dark time. They are a testament to the incredible man he was, and the impact he had on my life.

Tonight, as I lie in bed, I feel the weight of the day pressing down on me. The tears come easily, a release of the pent-up emotions that have been building all day. It's a relief, in a way, to let them out, to allow myself to feel the pain, to mourn the loss of someone so dear to me.

Je sais que le chemin à venir sera difficile. There will be many more tears, many more moments of sorrow. But I also know that I am not alone. I have my family, my memories, and the love of Grand-père Alain to guide me. It's a small comfort, but it's something to hold onto.

As I close my eyes, I try to focus on the good times, the happy memories. I think about the lessons he taught me, the laughter we shared, the bond we had. These thoughts bring a small smile to my face, a flicker of light in the darkness.

Il est tard, et je suis épuisée. The emotional toll of the day has left me drained, but also determined. I will carry on, for him, for myself. I will find a way to honour his memory, to live up to the expectations he had for me. It won't be easy, but I am determined to try.

Je t'aime, Grand-père Alain. You will always be in my heart, guiding me, inspiring me. Your legacy lives on in me, in everything I do. I will make you proud, I promise. Rest in peace, knowing that your love and wisdom continue to shape my life.

As I drift off to sleep, I feel a sense of calm wash over me. The pain is still there, but so is the love. And in that love, I find the strength to face another day.

Bon nuit,

Amèlie

Chapter 12: A New Beginning

It had been a few days since Grand-père Alain had passed away. The world felt a little dimmer, a little colder without his presence. Amélie had been grappling with a whirlwind of emotions since then. Her family had returned to Nice, and while the immediate shock had faded, the grief lingered like an unwelcome guest.

On this particular day, Amélie sought solace at a quiet spot overlooking the cliffs of Nice. The sun was high in the sky, casting a warm, golden light across the Mediterranean Sea. The gentle sound of waves crashing against the rocks provided a rhythmic background to her thoughts.

Amélie sat on a weathered wooden bench, her book resting in her lap. It was a novel she had picked up on a whim, something to distract her mind from the relentless ache of loss. The book's pages fluttered in the light breeze, but Amélie's focus was elsewhere. Her eyes were distant, staring out at the horizon, lost in thought.

Les jours passent en silence, chaque jour semblant plus lourd que le précédent. The void left by Grand-père Alain felt like an unfillable chasm. He had been a cornerstone in her life, his presence a constant source of comfort and guidance. Now, the only thing left were memories, and those were tinged with the sharp sting of finality.

She flipped through the pages of her book without really reading. The characters and their adventures felt inconsequential compared to the magnitude of her grief. She tried to focus on the words, to escape into a fictional world, but her mind kept drifting back to the scenes of the past week.

Il y avait tellement de gens qui sont venus rendre hommage à Grand-père Alain. Each person had a story to share, a memory to offer. The funeral had been a whirlwind of faces and voices, all united in their sorrow. Amélie had felt overwhelmed by the sheer volume of it all, the collective grief almost too much to bear.

Today was different. There were no crowds, no somber faces. It was just her, the sea, and the wind. Amélie took a deep breath, savoring the fresh, salty air. It was moments like these that offered her a brief respite from the storm of emotions.

The bench she sat on was one of her favorite spots, a place she had come to often when she needed to think or find solace. It was a place of quiet reflection, and today it served as a sanctuary from the tumultuous feelings that had been swirling inside her.

The day was calm, a stark contrast to the stormy days of grief she had experienced recently. The sun cast a warm glow over the landscape, and the sea sparkled in the sunlight. It was beautiful, almost too beautiful, and Amélie felt a pang of guilt for feeling anything other than sorrow.

Elle a fermé les yeux un moment, laissant le soleil caresser son visage. The warmth was comforting, a gentle reminder that life, despite its challenges, continued. It was a moment of peace amid the chaos, a reminder that even in the darkest times, there could still be moments of light.

Amélie thought about Grand-père Alain and the many lessons he had taught her. He had been a guiding light in her life, always encouraging her to pursue her dreams, to be the best version of herself. His words echoed in her mind, offering both comfort and a challenge. How could she honour his memory? How could she live a life that reflected the values he had instilled in her?

Les souvenirs de Grand-père Alain étaient à la fois doux et douloureux. She recalled the countless conversations they had shared, the advice he had given her, the way he had always believed in her even when she struggled to believe in herself. His passing had left a void, but it also left behind a legacy of love and wisdom.

Her thoughts were interrupted by the distant sound of footsteps. She turned her head to see her mother, Isabelle, approaching with a concerned look on her face. Isabelle had been trying her best to stay strong for the family, but Amélie knew that she, too, was struggling.

"Maman," Amélie said softly, trying to muster a smile.

Isabelle sat down beside her on the bench, her gaze following the same path across the sea that Amélie had been observing. "How are you holding up?" she asked gently.

Amélie shrugged. "It's been hard. Every day feels like a challenge."

Isabelle nodded, her expression reflecting the shared pain. "I know, sweetie. It's been hard for all of us. But we have each other, and we need to remember that. Grand-père Alain wouldn't want us to be consumed by our grief. He'd want us to live our lives fully, to find happiness and purpose."

Amélie took a deep breath, considering her mother's words. "I've been trying. It's just so difficult."

Isabelle placed a comforting hand on Amélie's shoulder. "It is difficult, and it's okay to feel that way. Grieving is a process, and it takes time. But we'll get through this together."

Amélie nodded, appreciating her mother's support. She had always admired Isabelle's strength, and it was a comfort to know that her mother was there for her, even as they both navigated their own paths through the grief.

As they sat together in silence, Amélie couldn't help but reflect on the future. Grand-père Alain's passing had left her with a sense of uncertainty, a feeling that her life was at a crossroads. She knew that she had to find a way to move forward, to honour his memory by living a life that reflected his values.

The warmth of the sun and the calm of the sea provided a sense of solace, but the path ahead still felt daunting. Amélie was determined to find her way, to discover what she wanted to do with her life now that Grand-père Alain was no longer there to guide her.

"I've been thinking," Amélie said, breaking the silence. "About what I want to do with my life. Grand-père Alain always encouraged me to pursue my dreams. I want to make sure that I do that, even though it feels difficult right now."

Isabelle looked at her with a mixture of pride and sadness. "He would be so proud of you, Amélie. I know he wanted you to achieve great things, and I have no doubt that you will. It's okay to take your time, to figure things out. But don't forget that he believed in you, and so do I."

Amélie smiled, feeling a sense of reassurance from her mother's words. "Thank you, Maman. It means a lot to me."

They sat together for a while longer, watching the sea and reflecting on the memories of Grand-père Alain. It was a peaceful moment, a reminder that despite the pain, there was still beauty in the world and hope for the future.

As the sun began to set, casting a warm, golden light over the landscape, Amélie felt a renewed sense of determination. She knew that the road ahead would be challenging, but she was ready to face it. Grand-père Alain's memory would always be with her, guiding her, inspiring her to be the best version of herself.

The chapter of her life that had been marked by grief and loss was ending, and a new chapter was beginning. It would be one filled with its own challenges and triumphs, but Amélie was ready to embrace it with an open heart. She would honour Grand-père Alain's legacy by living a life that reflected his love and wisdom.

As they made their way back home, Amélie felt a sense of peace. The journey ahead would not be easy, but it was a journey she was prepared to face. With her family by her side and the memory of Grand-père Alain guiding her, she knew that she could find her way.

Amélie's Diary

Today has been... different. It's been a few days since Grandpère Alain passed away, and the house has become a strange mix of silence and whispers. Everyone is trying to stay strong, but I can feel the sadness lingering in every room, like a heavy cloud that won't go away. C'est difficile to explain what I'm feeling. Sometimes I feel completely numb, like I'm just floating through the day without really being there. Other times, my emotions are so intense, they threaten to overwhelm me.

I've noticed that my mood swings are getting worse. One moment I'll be fine, reading a book or doing my homework, and then suddenly, without warning, I'm either incredibly angry or incredibly sad. C'est comme si je n'avais aucun contrôle sur mes émotions. I've been doing my best to manage these feelings, but it's not easy. It feels as though something inside me is shifting, like my mind is out of balance. I've heard people talk about bipolar disorder, and I can't help but wonder if I'm experiencing some of those symptoms.

It's difficult to talk to anyone about this. I don't want to burden anyone more than they already are. Mom and Dad have been so focused on trying to cope with the loss of Grandpère, and I know they're doing their best to support me. Mais je ne sais pas comment leur dire ce que je ressens. They seem to be dealing with their own grief, and I don't want to add to their worries.

I spent some time today sitting on the bench in the garden, trying to clear my mind. I had my book with me, a novel that's been my escape for a while now. Reading helps me forget, if only for a little while. It's a way to lose myself in another world, away from the pain and confusion of my own. But today, even that didn't seem to help much. I kept finding myself distracted, my mind drifting back to Grandpère and the strange, unsettling feelings I've been having.

I've been trying to stay busy, to focus on my studies and keep my mind occupied. It's my way of avoiding the emotions that I don't fully understand or know how to handle. C'est une distraction temporaire, mais ça m'aide à garder les choses sous contrôle, même si ce n'est que pour un moment.

Sometimes, when I'm alone, I catch myself crying for no apparent reason. It's not always a sadness I can pinpoint; it's more like an overwhelming sense of loss and confusion. Je me demande si je vais trouver un moyen de surmonter tout ça. I know it's okay to grieve, but this feeling of losing control is new and frightening.

I wish I could talk to someone who understands what I'm going through, but I don't even know how to start that conversation. I've been trying to write my thoughts down more often, hoping it might help me make sense of everything. Maybe, by putting my feelings into words, I can find a way to manage them better.

For now, I'll continue to read and write, and try to find some solace in the small things that bring me comfort. I know it won't be easy, and there will be days when the sadness feels overwhelming, but I have to keep going. I have to believe that things will get better eventually. C'est tout ce que je peux faire.

Maintenant, je suis fatigué. Je dois dormir.

Good night,

Amèlie Dubois

Chapter 13: The Unseen Path

The morning light filtered gently through the curtains of Amélie's room, casting a warm glow over her desk where various medical journals, textbooks, and sketches were strewn about. It was here, amidst the organized chaos of her workspace, that Amélie embarked on a new intellectual journey. Despite the recent grief she had endured, her mind remained sharp and focused, driven by an unyielding passion for medicine and discovery.

The days since Grandpère Alain's passing had been filled with a mix of grief and determination. While the house had become a quiet place of mourning, Amélie found solace in her academic pursuits. Her usual routine of excellence had become both a refuge and a battleground, where her genius could flourish even in the midst of personal turmoil.

Amélie's latest project was inspired by her ongoing studies and her desire to make a meaningful contribution to the medical field. Her focus had shifted to Meniere's disease, a condition she had encountered through her extensive reading. The disease, characterized by vertigo, hearing loss, and tinnitus, intrigued her due to its complex nature and the limited treatment options available.

Her desk was cluttered with research papers, anatomical diagrams, and sketches of potential solutions for Meniere's disease. Amélie's fingers moved swiftly over her notepad as she sketched out various surgical approaches. Her diagrams depicted intricate plans for a novel surgical procedure that she hoped could offer long-term relief to those suffering from the condition.

Amélie's idea was to design a surgical cure that would address the underlying causes of Meniere's disease rather than just managing its symptoms. The challenge was significant, but Amélie thrived on these kinds of intellectual puzzles. Her mind raced with possibilities, each more intriguing than the last.

Despite the complexity of her project, Amélie was determined to keep her discovery a secret. She had always been protective of her ideas, particularly those she considered groundbreaking. The thought of sharing her concept prematurely made her uneasy. She wanted to ensure that her design was fully developed and tested before presenting it to anyone.

The solitude of her room provided the perfect environment for her to concentrate. The soft hum of the desk lamp and the occasional rustling of papers were the only sounds accompanying her as she immersed herself in her work. Her sketches grew more detailed with each passing hour, and her excitement about the potential impact of her discovery grew.

Amélie's mother, Isabelle, knocked gently on the door before entering. "Amélie, dear, it's almost time for lunch. Don't you think you should take a break?"

Amélie looked up from her sketches, her eyes bright with enthusiasm. "I'm just working on something really important, Mum. I'm designing a surgical cure for Meniere's disease."

Isabelle's eyes widened in admiration. "That sounds incredible. I'm so proud of you for tackling such a challenging project."

"I'm excited about it," Amélie said. "But I need to keep working. I want to make sure everything is perfect before I share it with anyone."

Isabelle nodded, though a look of concern lingered in her eyes. "Just remember to take care of yourself, Amélie. It's important to find a balance."

"I will, Mum," Amélie replied, already turning her attention back to her work. "I'll come downstairs soon."

Amélie's Diary

Today, I spent most of my time in my room, diving deep into my project on Meniere's disease. It feels like the only thing that can really keep my mind off everything else. The house is quiet, and even though everyone's trying to support each other, it still feels so empty without Grandpère Alain. I guess it's just that I find comfort in my work, in creating something that might make a real difference.

I've been keeping my progress a secret, even from Mum. I know she'd be supportive, but there's something about this project that I want to keep to myself for now. I'm designing a surgical cure that I hope could help people suffering from Meniere's disease. I've read so much about it, and the idea of potentially offering a new solution is both thrilling and daunting.

My sketches are scattered across my desk, filled with intricate diagrams and detailed notes. I'm trying to create a small implantable device that could help regulate inner ear fluid balance, which seems to be a key issue in Meniere's disease. I want this device to be precise and effective. It's hard to explain, but when I'm working on this, I feel a sense of purpose and escape from the sadness. It's like my brain is in its own little world, far away from the grief that seems to hover over everything else.

Mum came in today and reminded me to take a break. She's always so thoughtful, but I'm so engrossed in my work that I barely notice the time passing. I promised her I'd come downstairs soon, but I ended up staying up in my room, refining my designs. It's strange, but even though I'm excited about the project, there's a part of me that's also scared. What if it doesn't work? What if I'm not as brilliant as I think I am? But then again, I have to try. It feels like this is something I'm meant to do.

I feel like I'm on the verge of something big, but I also feel a bit strange. Like, sometimes, I wonder if I'm not quite myself, if that makes any sense. The project helps, but there's a lingering sense of being out of balance, like I'm trying to hold everything together while feeling like I'm losing my grip on something important.

For now, I'll keep working on my design, and I'll keep it a secret until I'm ready. Maybe then it'll be ready to help others, and maybe it'll help me feel a little bit more grounded in all of this.

– Amélie

Chapter 14: Returning to Routine

The first day back at school felt like stepping into a different world for Amélie. The familiar surroundings were comforting, yet they felt strangely distant after the intense period of grief and adjustment she had recently experienced. The vibrant noise of students catching up with one another, the rustle of books and papers, and the smell of freshly sharpened pencils filled the air, creating a backdrop of normalcy that seemed almost foreign.

As Amélie walked through the school gates, she saw Philippe and Cécile waiting for her at their usual meeting spot near the entrance. Philippe's welcoming grin and Cécile's warm wave immediately brought a semblance of familiarity and comfort.

"Amélie! Ça fait si longtemps!" Philippe exclaimed, pulling her into a hug. "We missed you so much!"

Cécile chimed in, "Oui, nous avons hâte de rattraper le temps perdu! How was Paris?"

Amélie smiled, though a hint of sadness lingered in her eyes. "It was... overwhelming. But it's good to see you both."

Philippe and Cécile exchanged worried glances but said nothing further, respecting Amélie's space. They walked together into the school, chatting about their summer holidays and the latest school news.

As the day progressed, Amélie tried to immerse herself in her studies, attending classes and participating in discussions. However, the weight of her recent experiences seemed to hover over her. The comfort of the school environment was a stark contrast to the turmoil she had been through, and it took effort to stay focused on her academic responsibilities.

During the break between lessons, Amélie found herself in the cafeteria, where Philippe and Cécile joined her for lunch. They chatted about school projects and upcoming events, trying to keep the conversation light and positive. Despite their efforts, Amélie's thoughts often drifted to the recent past.

Later in the day, Amélie and Alex were summoned to the staff room by Monsieur Lefebvre, their history teacher. Monsieur Lefebvre was known for his deep passion for history and his attentive nature toward his students. The walls of his office were adorned with historical maps and artifacts, creating an atmosphere of scholarly curiosity.

"Amélie, Alex, come in," Monsieur Lefebvre called as they entered the room. His expression was a mix of concern and kindness.

They took their seats, and Monsieur Lefebvre looked at them thoughtfully. "I wanted to check in with both of you about how you're adjusting back to school."

Alex shifted uncomfortably. "It's been tough, but we're managing."

Monsieur Lefebvre nodded understandingly. "I can imagine. Returning to a normal routine after such a difficult period is never easy. If you need any support, academic or personal, please let me know."

Amélie nodded, though she felt a pang of vulnerability. "We're doing our best. It's just... a lot to handle."

Monsieur Lefebvre's gaze softened as he turned to Amélie. "Amélie, can we talk privately for a moment?"

Alex gave Amélie a reassuring nod before exiting the room, leaving her alone with Monsieur Lefebvre. The teacher's expression was earnest as he gestured for her to sit down again.

"Amélie," he began gently, "I've noticed that you've been more withdrawn lately. I want to make sure you're doing okay and to discuss how we can support you during this transition."

Amélie took a deep breath, feeling a mix of relief and apprehension. "I've been working on a new project to keep myself occupied. It helps distract me from everything that's happened, but sometimes I feel... not quite myself."

Monsieur Lefebvre leaned forward, his tone empathetic. "It's normal to feel that way, especially after such a significant loss. I'm glad you have something to focus on, but it's also important to address how you're feeling overall."

Amélie nodded, her voice trembling slightly. "I'm trying to stay strong, but it's hard. I don't want to let anyone down."

"Amélie," Monsieur Lefebvre said softly, "it's important to take care of yourself. You're doing a lot by managing your studies and dealing with personal challenges. Sometimes, it's okay to take a step back and find a balance."

Amélie looked at him, feeling a sense of gratitude for his understanding. "I just want to make sure I'm doing everything right."

Monsieur Lefebvre smiled reassuringly. "You're doing more than enough. It's important to balance your academic responsibilities with self-care. If you need a break or any adjustments to your workload, please let me know. Your well-being is important."

Amélie felt a wave of relief wash over her. "Thank you, Monsieur Lefebvre. I appreciate your support."

He nodded, his expression kind. "Remember, it's okay to seek help and take time for yourself. We're here to support you."

As Amélie left the staff room, she felt a renewed sense of hope. The conversation with Monsieur Lefebvre had been comforting, and his words provided reassurance. She returned to her classroom where Philippe and Cécile were waiting for her.

"Everything okay?" Philippe asked, noticing her thoughtful expression.

Amélie smiled, though it was tinged with sadness. "Yes, I just needed to talk to Monsieur Lefebvre. He's been really understanding."

Cécile reached out and gave her a gentle pat on the back. "We're here for you, Amélie. Anytime you need us."

"Thank you," Amélie said, feeling grateful for their support. "It means a lot to me."

As the day continued, Amélie tried to focus on her lessons, but her thoughts often wandered. The comfort of her friends and the routine of school were helping her adjust, but the pain of her recent loss was still fresh.

The day ended with Amélie walking home, reflecting on the conversations she had with Monsieur Lefebvre and her friends. She felt a mixture of hope and apprehension as she faced the challenges ahead. The support of those around her was a source of strength, and she was determined to find a balance between her grief and her responsibilities.

Amélie's Diary

Today was a significant day. After a period of grieving and adjustment, I finally returned to school. The whole experience felt surreal, a mix of familiarity and strangeness. Walking through those gates again, I saw Philippe and Cécile waiting for me, their faces lighting up with joy. Philippe's enthusiastic greeting and Cécile's warm hug made me feel a bit more at ease.

Even so, as the day went on, the routine of school felt jarring. The bustling energy of the school, the chatter of students, and the familiar smell of textbooks seemed almost too bright and overwhelming. It's as if the world moved on while I was stuck in a pause.

During our break, I found some comfort in chatting with Philippe and Cécile. We talked about our summer, what we'd missed, and how everything had changed. They were so understanding, trying to keep things light and supportive. Their presence was reassuring, but I couldn't shake off the heaviness in my heart.

Monsieur Lefebvre, our history teacher, asked to speak with Alex and me. I felt a knot in my stomach as we walked to his office. The staff room was decorated with historical artifacts, a reminder of the world beyond our own troubles. Monsieur Lefebvre greeted us with a kind, yet concerned look.

He began the conversation by asking how we were adjusting back to school. Alex and I exchanged glances, both of us struggling to articulate our feelings. I mentioned that we were trying our best but that it was challenging. Monsieur Lefebvre listened attentively, his concern evident.

Then he asked to speak with me alone. I was nervous but also relieved. His office, filled with the smell of old books and polished wood, felt like a haven where I could openly express my feelings. Monsieur Lefebvre's compassionate demeanour made it easier to talk about how I was struggling.

He told me that it's normal to feel overwhelmed after such a significant loss. He encouraged me to take care of myself and find a balance. His words were comforting, reminding me that it's okay to take breaks and not push myself too hard. I appreciated his support and felt a bit lighter after our conversation.

Later, Philippe and Cécile joined me for the rest of the day. They were attentive and tried to keep my spirits up. Despite their efforts, I found it difficult to focus on my studies. My thoughts often wandered to the recent past, and the weight of my emotions made it hard to concentrate.

When I walked home, I reflected on the day. The comfort of school and the support of friends were helping me, but the grief still lingered. I was trying to find a balance between my responsibilities and taking care of my emotional well-being.

I'm still grappling with the feelings of sadness and the strange sensation of not quite being myself. It's a mix of emotions that I'm trying to navigate, one step at a time. I'm hopeful that, with time, things will start to feel more manageable.

— Amélie

Chapter 15: The Maths Competition

The atmosphere in the school hall was charged with a palpable excitement. The annual maths competition was one of the most anticipated events of the year, and students from various classes had come together to test their logical and mathematical prowess. The hall was decorated with colourful banners and motivational posters, creating an environment that buzzed with competitive energy.

Amélie sat at her desk, her mind oscillating between the task at hand and the recent loss of her grandfather. The grief still weighed heavily on her, and it was difficult to keep her focus. Despite this, she was determined to participate in the competition. The memory of Alain was a driving force behind her will to perform well, even though the pain often felt overwhelming.

The competition began with a signal from the organiser, and students were handed their question papers. Each paper contained 25 logical and mathematical problems, each worth 5 marks. The challenge was as much about speed as it was about accuracy. Amélie's fingers trembled slightly as she opened her paper, but she quickly forced herself to focus on the first question.

As she worked through the questions, Amélie tried to push aside the ache in her heart. The pain of losing Alain was something she could not ignore, and it often distracted her from the task at hand. She knew that the competition was a way to channel her energy and perhaps find a temporary reprieve from her grief. The familiar challenge of solving mathematical problems provided a sense of normalcy amidst the chaos of her emotions.

Across the room, Nadine, one of Amélie's classmates and an unkind rival, was also participating. Nadine had always been dismissive and sometimes outright hostile towards Amélie. The rivalry between them was a source of tension, and Nadine's presence in the competition added an extra layer of pressure for Amélie. The sight of Nadine, who had always been eager to prove herself superior, was a reminder of the unkindness Amélie had endured.

The clock ticked away, and Amélie remained engrossed in solving each problem. Her mind was sharp despite the turmoil, and she was determined to do her best. However, as the competition drew to a close, she couldn't help but feel a pang of worry. The questions had been challenging, and she hoped that her performance had been enough to secure a good position.

Finally, the time was up, and the papers were collected. The hall filled with a murmur of anticipation as students waited for the results. Amélie tried to remain composed, but her heart raced with anxiety. The competition had been intense, and she knew that the margin for error was slim.

After what seemed like an eternity, the results were announced. The organiser stepped onto the stage and began calling out names, starting with the top scorers. When Nadine's name was called out first, a cheer erupted from her friends. Amélie felt a sinking feeling in her stomach as she listened to the results.

"Nadine takes the first place with 120 marks," the organiser announced. "Amélie comes in second with 119 marks."

The words felt like a blow to Amélie's heart. She had come so close but had been narrowly beaten by Nadine. Despite her strong performance, the loss stung deeply. The competition, which was supposed to be a testament to her skills, had now become a reminder of her recent struggles and the sense of inadequacy she felt.

Nadine, with a smug smile on her face, wasted no time in spreading a cruel rumour about Amélie. She insinuated that Amélie's near victory was a fluke and that she had only performed well due to luck. The rumour quickly spread through the school, and Amélie found herself at the centre of unwanted attention.

The weight of Nadine's words and the loss of her grandfather combined to create an emotional burden that felt almost unbearable.

Amélie's feelings of sadness were compounded by the harshness of Nadine's taunts. It felt like a part of her had been torn away, leaving her vulnerable and exposed.

Despite the hurtful rumours and her internal struggle, Amélie was not alone. Her friends—Alex, Philippe, and Cécile—rallied around her, offering their support and comfort. Alex, despite his occasional teasing, was genuinely concerned and did his best to lift her spirits. Philippe and Cécile, always compassionate, provided a listening ear and words of encouragement.

The teachers also played a crucial role in supporting Amélie. Monsieur Lefebvre, in particular, took her aside after the competition to offer his reassurance. He spoke to her in private, acknowledging her effort and reminding her of her abilities. His words were a balm to her wounded spirit, and she felt a flicker of hope in his encouragement.

In the aftermath of the competition, Amélie's friends and teachers helped her navigate the difficult emotions she was experiencing. They reminded her of her strengths and achievements, providing a counterbalance to the negativity she had faced. The kindness and understanding of those around her became a source of solace during a challenging time.

As the day ended, Amélie reflected on the competition and its aftermath. Despite the disappointment and the cruel rumours, she found strength in the support she received. The road to recovery and acceptance would be long, but she was determined to move forward with resilience and grace.

The competition had tested her not only academically but emotionally. Amélie's journey through grief and adversity had shaped her into a more resilient person. With the support of her friends and the encouragement of her teachers, she was ready to face the future, no matter how daunting it might seem.

The day concluded with a mix of emotions. The sting of defeat was still present, but it was softened by the warmth of friendship and the strength of character that had emerged from her trials. Amélie knew that she would carry on, using her experiences to grow and continue striving for excellence in all areas of her life.

Amélie's Diary

I don't know how to start this entry. It's been a really hard day, and I feel like I'm falling apart inside. I'm trying to be strong, but it's getting so hard. I wish things were different, but they're not. I wish I could just wake up and find everything back to how it was before Grand-père Alain passed away.

The maths competition today was supposed to be something I could focus on, a way to push away the pain and just concentrate on something I was good at. But now it feels like it was a cruel joke. I was so determined to do well, to make Grand-père Alain proud, and I came so close to winning. I gave it everything I had, and yet it wasn't enough. I got second place, just one mark behind Nadine.

Nadine. I don't even want to think about her. She's always been horrible to me, and today she just had to rub it in my face. When she won, I felt like a part of me was torn away. And then, to make things worse, she started spreading rumours about me. She told everyone that my second-place finish was just luck, that I didn't deserve it. It's like she wanted to take everything from me, not just the competition but my dignity too.

The pain of losing Grand-père Alain is still fresh, and now this defeat feels like another blow. It's not just about the competition, it's about everything that's been happening. I've been trying so hard to stay focused and do well, but it seems like no matter how hard I try, I can't escape this feeling of being torn apart.

I spent most of the day trying to hold back tears, trying to pretend that everything was okay. I was with my friends—Alex, Philippe, and Cécile—and they tried their best to cheer me up. Alex, who can be so insensitive sometimes, was actually really supportive. He must have noticed how upset I was and tried to make me laugh. Philippe and Cécile were there too, offering their comforting words and just being there for me. I'm grateful for their support, but it doesn't change how empty I feel inside.

Monsieur Lefebvre talked to me after the competition. He's always been one of the few teachers who understands me, and he tried to reassure me. He told me that I did well and that I should be proud of myself, but it's hard to feel proud when all I can think about is how close I was to winning and how it didn't happen. His words were kind, but they didn't take away the pain. They didn't fix the hurt that Nadine's rumours have caused.

The whole day felt like a whirlwind. I could barely focus on anything, and even when I tried to do something normal, like reading or doing homework, my mind kept wandering back to how awful everything feels. It's like I'm stuck in a loop of sadness, and every attempt to break free only makes the pain worse.

I want to scream and cry and just let everything out, but I don't know how. I feel so lost, like I'm drifting in a sea of sadness with no way to find my way back. Grand-père Alain's death has left such a huge hole in my life, and now it feels like the competition and Nadine's cruelty have just made everything worse.

I keep thinking about how things used to be, how simple and happy everything was before all of this happened. I miss Grand-père Alain so much. I miss his voice, his laughter, and the way he used to make me feel safe. I miss the days when I didn't have to worry about competing and losing and dealing with people who want to bring me down.

I feel like a part of me is missing, and I don't know how to get it back. I know that life goes on, and that I have to keep moving forward, but it's so hard when everything feels so empty. I keep trying to remind myself that I have people who care about me, that I have friends and family who support me. But right now, it doesn't feel like enough.

I wish I could just forget about today and all the pain it brought. I wish I could find a way to be happy again, to feel like myself. But right now, it's hard to see past the sadness and the hurt. I'm trying to stay strong, to keep going despite everything, but it's like walking through a fog of sorrow that never seems to lift.

I just want to feel normal again, to have a day where I'm not weighed down by grief and disappointment. I want to be able to enjoy the things I used to love without this constant ache in my heart. I want to find a way to move forward, but right now, it feels impossible.

I don't know what the future holds, and that scares me. I don't know how to handle all of this pain and sadness, and I don't know if I'll ever be able to truly move on from it. I'm trying my best, but it feels like my best isn't enough.

I miss Grand-père Alain more than words can say. I wish he was here to tell me that everything will be okay, to make me feel better. But he's not here, and I have to find a way to deal with all of this on my own. It's the hardest thing I've ever had to do, and I don't know if I'm strong enough to handle it.

I hope that someday things will get better, that I'll find a way to heal and move forward. But for now, all I can do is try to get through each day, one step at a time. I'm holding onto the hope that things will eventually improve, but it's hard to keep that hope alive when everything feels so bleak.

I just want to be able to smile again, to find joy in life despite all the pain. I want to be able to look back on today and see it as a moment of struggle that I overcame, not just another chapter in a story of sadness.

But for now, I'm still trying to find my way through this fog of sorrow. I'm still trying to find a reason to keep going, to keep pushing forward despite the pain. I don't know what the future holds, but I'm holding onto the hope that things will get better.

For now, I'm signing off with a heavy heart and a mind full of sadness. I'm hoping that tomorrow will be a better day, and that I'll find a way to move past all of this hurt.

— Amélie

Chapter 16: The Turning Point

Amélie sat at her desk, staring blankly at her math workbook. The events of the past weeks weighed heavily on her. The loss of her grandfather, Alain, still a fresh wound, was something she couldn't shake off. The pain from the math competition was still lingering, and Nadine's hurtful rumours had chipped away at her confidence. Despite her efforts to focus, the numbers and equations seemed like a foreign language.

Monsieur Lefebvre had noticed her struggles. He had always been a perceptive teacher, someone who saw beyond the surface of his students' lives. He knew Amélie was a brilliant student, but he could also see the toll the past few weeks had taken on her. After class one day, he called her over.

"Amélie," he began, his voice gentle yet firm, "I've noticed that you haven't been yourself lately. I'm concerned about you. You're carrying a lot on your shoulders, and it's affecting your work."

Amélie nodded, not trusting herself to speak. Her throat felt tight, and tears pricked at the corners of her eyes.

"I understand that you're going through a difficult time," Monsieur Lefebvre continued. "But I want you to remember that it's okay to take a break. You're an extraordinary student, Amélie, but you're also human. You need balance in your life, especially now."

Amélie looked up at him, her eyes filled with a mixture of gratitude and sadness. "But I don't want to fall behind," she whispered. "Math is the only thing that makes sense to me right now."

Monsieur Lefebvre smiled softly. "Math will always be there, Amélie. But you need to take care of yourself too. Sometimes, stepping back is the best way to move forward."

The conversation stayed with Amélie for days. She thought about it during class, while walking to and from school, and even as she lay in bed at night. Monsieur Lefebvre's words had struck a chord deep within her. She knew he was right—she needed to find a way to balance her life, to give herself permission to grieve, to rest, and to heal.

One afternoon, after a particularly exhausting day at school, Amélie decided to visit her favorite spot by the river. It was a place where she had always felt at peace, where she could think clearly. The river was partially frozen, the surface glistening in the fading sunlight. She sat on a bench, pulling her coat tighter around her to keep warm, and stared out at the water.

Philippe and Cécile had been supportive throughout everything. They had stood by her side during the competition, offering words of encouragement and comfort when she needed them most. Their friendship was one of the few things that brought her solace, and she was grateful for their presence in her life.

As Amélie watched the river, she thought about the future. She knew that the road ahead wouldn't be easy, but she also knew that she had the strength to face whatever came her way. Alain's death had left a void in her life, but it had also given her a new perspective. Life was precious, and she didn't want to waste any more time dwelling on the past.

A week later, Monsieur Lefebvre announced a new project for the class. It was a group assignment, focused on creating a mathematical model for a real-world problem. The project excited Amélie—math had always been her escape, and this was the perfect opportunity to immerse herself in something productive.

She was paired with Philippe and Cécile, and together they brainstormed ideas for their project. They decided to focus on environmental sustainability, creating a model to predict the impact of pollution on local ecosystems. It was a challenging task, but one that Amélie threw herself into with renewed vigour.

Working on the project helped Amélie reconnect with the things she loved. The calculations, the problem-solving, the collaborative effort—it all reminded her of why she had fallen in love with math in the first place. For the first time in weeks, she felt a sense of purpose, a drive to succeed.

But the healing process wasn't linear. There were still moments when the grief would overwhelm her, when she would feel like she was drowning in sorrow. During those times, she would find herself thinking about Alain, about the lessons he had taught her, about the love and wisdom he had imparted. She would cry, letting the tears flow freely, knowing that it was all part of the process.

Philippe and Cécile were there for her during those difficult moments. They never pushed her to talk, but their presence was a comfort. They would sit with her, sometimes in silence, sometimes sharing memories or simply making her laugh. They understood that she needed time, that healing couldn't be rushed.

As the weeks passed, Amélie began to feel a shift within herself. The pain was still there, but it was no longer all-consuming. She could think about Alain without breaking down, could remember the good times they had shared without being overwhelmed by grief. She knew that she would always miss him, but she also knew that he would want her to live her life to the fullest.

The project became a turning point for Amélie. She poured her energy into it, working late into the night, refining the model, ensuring that every detail was perfect. Monsieur Lefebvre was impressed with their progress, and his praise gave Amélie a much-needed boost of confidence.

On the day of the presentation, Amélie stood in front of the class, her heart pounding in her chest. She felt a mix of nerves and excitement, but as she began to speak, she found her voice. The words flowed naturally, and as she explained the intricacies of their model, she felt a sense of pride.

When the presentation was over, the class erupted in applause. Philippe and Cécile beamed at her, and even Monsieur Lefebvre looked pleased. Amélie smiled, a genuine smile that reached her eyes. It was a small victory, but one that marked a significant step in her journey of healing.

As the school day ended, Amélie walked home with a lighter heart. She knew that there would still be challenges ahead, that there would be days when the grief would resurface. But she also knew that she had the strength to overcome those challenges, to find her way forward.

The conversation with Monsieur Lefebvre had been a turning point for her, a reminder that it was okay to take a step back, to prioritize her well-being. And as she continued on her journey, she knew that she would carry those lessons with her, finding balance in a world that often felt overwhelming.

Life was beginning to look a little brighter for Amélie. The future was still uncertain, but for the first time in a long while, she felt hopeful. She knew that she wasn't alone, that she had the support of her friends and family, and that she had the strength within herself to face whatever challenges lay ahead.

Amélie's journey was far from over, but she was ready to face it head-on, armed with the lessons she had learned and the love of those who cared about her. And as she looked up at the sky, the sun beginning to set, she knew that, no matter what, she would find her way.

Amélie's Diary

Today was a day of emotions, swirling and intense. I woke up feeling a strange mix of sadness and determination, as if the world was both against me and pushing me forward. It's hard to describe, but there's this sense of being caught in a storm, where the winds pull me in different directions, and I can't quite find my footing.

Monsieur Lefebvre noticed right away. His eyes, toujours si perçants, seemed to see through me as if he could understand the turmoil I was trying to hide. He asked me how I was doing, and I could only manage a small shrug, unable to put everything I was feeling into words. He didn't press, but I could tell he was concerned.

The competition today was another blow. I knew it wouldn't be easy, but I didn't expect to feel so defeated by the end of it. Nadine, with her smug smile and condescending tone, made sure to rub it in that she had won. It wasn't just that she beat me by one point—it was the way she gloated, spreading rumours about my loss as if it defined who I am. I wanted to scream, to tell her that it wasn't just about the competition, that I had so much more on my mind, but the words stuck in my throat.

Pourquoi doit-elle toujours être si crueller? Why does she always have to be so cruel? It's like she finds joy in my pain, and I can't understand it. I try to remind myself that her words don't define me, that I am more than just one competition, but it's hard when everyone around you seems to believe the lies she spreads.

Philippe and Cécile were there for me, like they always are. Their support means the world to me, but even their kindness couldn't completely erase the sting of today's events. Philippe tried to make me laugh, telling silly jokes that usually work, but my heart just wasn't in it. Cécile gave me a hug, whispering that everything would be okay, and for a moment, I almost believed her. But the weight of everything just feels too heavy.

I think back to Grand-père Alain and how he would have encouraged me, telling me not to let this get to me, that life is full of challenges and it's how we face them that matters. But he's not here anymore, and that reality hits me harder every day. There's an emptiness that his absence has left, a void that I'm not sure will ever be filled.

Monsieur Lefebvre talked to me after class. He said I looked tired, and that maybe I should consider taking a break, finding some balance. I know he's right, but the idea of slowing down feels like giving up. I don't want to stop, because if I stop, then the pain will catch up to me, and I'm not sure I'm ready to face it head-on.

But what if I'm pushing too hard? What if, in trying to escape the sadness, I'm only making it worse? It's a thought that lingers in the back of my mind, gnawing at me whenever I try to focus on something else. Maybe Monsieur Lefebvre is right. Maybe I do need to take a step back, to breathe, to let myself grieve properly.

Je me sens perdue. I feel lost. There's no other way to describe it. I'm trying to keep up with everything, to maintain the façade that I'm okay, but inside, it's like I'm breaking apart piece by piece. I don't want to disappoint anyone, but I also don't know how much longer I can keep pretending that I'm fine.

The tears came easily tonight, as I sat alone in my room. It's become a ritual, almost—holding everything in until I'm alone, and then letting it all out in the silence of my own space. I wish I could be stronger, that I could just brush off the hurtful words and the disappointments, but I'm not there yet. Maybe one day I will be, but today is not that day.

I know I should talk to someone about how I'm feeling, but the words don't come. It's easier to write them down, to let these pages hold my pain and my fears, than to say them out loud. Writing is my escape, my way of making sense of everything when nothing seems to make sense at all.

Tomorrow is a new day, but tonight, I'll let myself feel everything. The sadness, the anger, the frustration—they're all a part of me right now, and maybe that's okay. Maybe, with time, I'll learn to navigate these feelings, to find my way back to some semblance of normalcy. But for now, I'll take it one step at a time, one breath at a time, and hope that eventually, things will start to get better.

Amélie

Chapter 17: Resilience

As the days passed, the weight of everything—her grandfather's passing, the rumours, the pressures—remained heavy on Amélie's heart.

The night before, Amélie sat by her window, staring out at the dark Parisian skyline, her mind swimming with thoughts. She had always found solace in the quiet of the night, but lately, even that had been taken from her. Each time she closed her eyes, her thoughts raced, refusing to let her rest. It was as if her mind was a storm, tossing her emotions around with no mercy. She felt as if she were caught between the pressure of living up to everyone's expectations and the overwhelming grief that had been gnawing at her since her grandfather's death.

Peut-être que je ne suis pas assez forte (Maybe I'm not strong enough), she thought, her fingers tracing the edges of the medical journals she kept by her bedside. She hadn't opened them in days, unable to focus on anything other than the swirl of emotions inside her.

The next morning, as the sun began to rise, Amélie found herself drawn to her parents' room. François and Isabelle were still asleep, their faces relaxed and peaceful in a way that felt almost foreign to Amélie. It had been a while since she had seen them so calm, so untouched by the worries that weighed on her.

She quietly slipped out of the room and made her way downstairs. The house was eerily quiet, with only the soft hum of the refrigerator breaking the silence. Amélie headed to the kitchen, intending to prepare something to eat, but found herself instead standing in front of the large mirror by the entrance.

Qu'est-ce que je fais ici? (What am I doing here?), she wondered as she stared at her reflection. The girl looking back at her seemed tired—exhausted even. Her eyes were dull, her posture slumped. This was not the Amélie she used to be, the one who had always been so full of life and energy, who had thrown herself into her studies and her passions with relentless determination.

But that girl felt distant now, like a memory from another lifetime.

The day passed slowly. Amélie tried to engage in her usual activities, but nothing felt right. She even attempted to read one of her favorite books, something that had always brought her comfort, but the words seemed jumbled and meaningless. The sentences blurred together, and after a few pages, she closed the book in frustration, her heart sinking even lower.

As the afternoon sun streamed through the windows, casting a warm glow on the walls, Amélie found herself gravitating toward the piano in the living room. She hadn't played in months—hadn't even touched the keys since before Alain fell ill. But now, as she sat down on the bench, her fingers seemed to move on their own, lightly brushing the keys as if searching for something familiar.

The melody that came was soft, almost tentative, as if she were afraid of breaking something fragile. It wasn't a song she recognized, but rather something that flowed from deep within her, an outpouring of everything she had been holding back for so long. The notes were gentle at first, then gradually grew louder, more insistent, until the room was filled with a sound that was both mournful and beautiful.

As she played, she felt something inside her begin to shift. The weight that had been pressing down on her chest seemed to lift, just a little, and for the first time in days, she could breathe again. The music wasn't a solution to her problems, but it was a release—a way to express what she couldn't put into words.

When the last note faded into silence, Amélie sat back, her hands trembling slightly. She felt a tear slip down her cheek, followed by another, and soon she was crying, her shoulders shaking as she let out everything she had been holding in.

Je suis tellement fatiguée (I'm so tired), she thought, pressing the heels of her hands to her eyes. *Fatiguée de toujours devoir être forte, fatiguée de toujours devoir sourire, fatiguée de cette douleur qui ne s'en va pas* (Tired of always having to be strong, tired of always having to smile, tired of this pain that won't go away).

She didn't know how long she sat there, but eventually, the tears slowed, and she was left with a sense of calm she hadn't felt in a long time. The pain was still there, but it was no longer all-consuming. For the first time in weeks, Amélie felt like she could start to heal.

Just as she was about to leave the piano, she heard footsteps behind her. She turned to see Alex standing in the doorway, his expression soft with concern. He had always been the protective older brother, but lately, with everything that had happened, they had drifted apart.

"Amélie," he said quietly, stepping into the room. "I heard you playing."

She nodded, not trusting herself to speak without breaking down again. Alex came over and sat next to her on the piano bench. For a moment, they sat in silence, the only sound being the distant chirping of birds outside.

"I've been worried about you," Alex finally said, his voice low. "You've been so distant... I didn't know how to help."

Amélie looked down at her hands, the tears threatening to spill again. "I didn't know how to ask for help," she admitted, her voice barely above a whisper. "I felt like I had to be strong... for everyone."

"You don't always have to be strong," Alex said gently, placing a hand on her shoulder. "It's okay to lean on someone else when you need to."

Amélie took a shaky breath, the weight of his words sinking in. She had been so focused on being the perfect student, the perfect daughter, that she had forgotten it was okay to be vulnerable. That it was okay to let someone else carry the burden, even if just for a little while.

"I miss him so much," she whispered, her voice breaking. "I miss grand-père."

"I do too," Alex said, his voice thick with emotion. "But we'll get through this together, okay? You're not alone, Amélie."

For the first time in what felt like forever, Amélie allowed herself to believe those words. She leaned into her brother's embrace, letting the warmth of his presence soothe her aching heart. The pain was still there, but with Alex by her side, it felt just a little more bearable.

And as they sat there, side by side on the piano bench, Amélie knew that she didn't have to face the world alone. Together, they could find the strength to move forward, to heal, and to honour the memory of their grandfather in the best way they knew how—by living with love, courage, and resilience.

Amélie's diary

Cher Journal,

Today has been another challenging day. I woke up feeling the weight of yesterday's grief still hanging over me. It's like a thick fog that refuses to lift, making everything seem distant and unreal. I tried to focus on my work and my studies, but the sadness is always just beneath the surface, ready to break through.

I'm trying hard to keep myself together. I spent most of the morning working on my Meniere's disease surgical cure. It's a project that has become my refuge, a way to channel my thoughts and emotions into something constructive. When I'm working on it, I can almost forget the heaviness of my heart. It's a way to keep Grandfather's memory alive, to honour him by pursuing something he would have been proud of.

I've kept my discovery a secret for now. It's not because I'm worried about others knowing but because I need to focus without distractions. I feel like if I share it too soon, the pressure to perform and the scrutiny might affect my concentration. This work is my sanctuary, a place where I can escape from the noise and chaos of my emotions.

Sometimes, when I'm alone, I let myself feel the full weight of the loss. It's hard to admit, but I feel like a part of me has been torn away. Grandfather was such a huge part of my life, and his absence is like a gaping hole. I think about his last words often: "*I love you and will forever be in your hearts*." Those words are both a comfort and a reminder of his absence. They echo in my mind, and every time I think of them, I can't help but feel a pang of sorrow.

Alex has been trying his best to be supportive. He's been around, offering his help and trying to cheer me up. I know he's going through his own struggles, and sometimes it feels like we're both trying to stay afloat in a sea of grief. Despite our differences, he's shown me that he cares, and I'm grateful for that. He's been a rock in his own way, even if it's sometimes difficult to talk openly about our feelings.

The other day, I overheard a conversation among some of our friends and cousins. It wasn't a pleasant conversation, and it made me feel even more isolated. It's like I'm on the outside looking in, trying to understand where I fit in all of this. But I try not to let it affect me too much. I have to remind myself that I'm doing my best, and that's all I can ask for.

I've been working on my studies as well, trying to keep up with schoolwork despite everything. It's a way to keep my mind occupied and to avoid dwelling on the sadness. But even with the distraction of studies and projects, there are moments when the grief feels overwhelming. I find myself caught between wanting to push forward and feeling completely stuck.

In the evenings, I often find myself reading or working on the surgical design. Reading helps me escape for a while, and working on my project gives me a sense of purpose. It's during these quiet moments that I allow myself to reflect and remember Grandfather. I think about the times we spent together, the conversations we had, and the lessons he taught me. Those memories are precious, and they keep me grounded, even when everything else feels uncertain.

Tonight, I sat down to write this diary entry and found myself reflecting on the past few weeks. It's been a whirlwind of emotions, from the initial shock of Grandfather's passing to the slow process of coming to terms with the loss. It feels like every day is a new challenge, but I'm trying to face it with as much strength as I can muster.

I'm also trying to take care of myself. It's easy to get lost in the work and the sadness, but I know it's important to find a balance. I try to take breaks, to do things that make me happy, and to connect with the people who care about me. It's a small comfort in the midst of the pain, but it's something I hold onto.

As I finish this entry, I'm reminded of the importance of keeping Grandfather's memory alive. It's a way to honour him and to find a sense of peace amid the grief. I know that he would want me to keep going, to pursue my passions, and to live a life that reflects the values he instilled in me.

So, I'll keep moving forward, even if it feels like a slow and painful process. I'll hold onto the memories, the love, and the lessons he gave me. And I'll keep working on my projects, finding solace in the things that bring me joy and purpose.

Amélie

Chapter 18: The Dawn of New Horizon

Winter's grip was starting to loosen, but the chilly air of the early months lingered, reflecting the somber mood that still enveloped Amélie. As the days gradually lengthened, promising the arrival of spring, Amélie found herself caught in a whirlwind of emotions, struggling to adjust to the new rhythm of life without Grandfather Alain.

The house had a quiet that was almost tangible—a silence that spoke of the absence of Alain's laughter and wisdom. His presence had always been a steadying force for Amélie, and without him, the days seemed to blend into one another. Her focus had shifted from the bustling activity of school to the solitude of her room, where she buried herself in her work, hoping to find solace in the familiar comfort of her research.

Amélie's study had become her refuge. The walls were adorned with charts and diagrams, reflecting her dedication to her project on Meniere's disease. Despite the clarity of her research, she struggled to maintain the same level of enthusiasm. The weight of her grandfather's passing pressed heavily on her, adding a layer of emotional complexity to her scientific pursuits.

One particularly cold afternoon, as the sun dipped low in the sky, Amélie was deep in her research when Alex entered the room. He had been trying to be more present, offering support and companionship as she navigated through her grief and academic challenges.

"Hey, Amélie," Alex said softly, entering the study and pulling up a chair beside her desk. "How's everything going with the project?"

Amélie glanced up from her work, her eyes showing signs of exhaustion. "It's going. Slowly. I'm working on refining the surgical model, but it feels like I'm getting nowhere fast."

Alex could see the strain on her face. "I know this has been tough on you. You're doing incredible work, but you also need to take care of yourself. It's okay to step away for a bit."

Amélie appreciated his concern but felt a pang of guilt. "I just feel like I need to keep going. Grandfather believed in me so much, and I want to make sure his legacy lives on."

Alex nodded, understanding her sentiment but also worried about her well-being. "I get that, but you're only human. Even the most dedicated people need to take a break now and then. Why don't we go for a walk? Some fresh air might do you good."

Amélie hesitated, but the kindness in Alex's eyes was convincing. "Alright, a walk sounds nice."

They stepped outside, the crisp winter air filling their lungs. As they walked through the neighbourhood, the first hints of spring were beginning to show. Tiny buds were starting to appear on the trees, and the snow was melting away, revealing patches of green beneath. The changing season seemed to mirror Amélie's internal shift, offering a glimmer of hope amidst her sorrow.

The siblings walked in companionable silence, occasionally breaking it with light conversation. Alex shared anecdotes from school, and Amélie found herself laughing at his stories, if only for a moment. The weight of her grief seemed a little lighter, if just for the duration of their walk.

Later that evening, as they returned home, Amélie felt a sense of renewed clarity. The simple act of taking a break had reminded her that she didn't have to bear her burdens alone. She returned to her room with a new perspective, deciding to incorporate regular breaks into her schedule and to be kinder to herself.

The following days brought a mix of routine and reflection. Amélie continued to work on her project but made a conscious effort to balance her time with moments of rest and self-care. She took up new hobbies, including sketching and reading novels, to provide a respite from her intense focus on her research.

One afternoon, Amélie found herself sitting at her desk, surrounded by textbooks and notes, when she received a message from Philippe and Cécile. They wanted to catch up and invited her to join them for a casual outing. The idea of spending time with friends was a welcome distraction, and Amélie accepted eagerly.

The three friends met at a cozy café in town. Philippe and Cécile greeted her with warm smiles, and their presence provided a much-needed sense of normalcy. They chatted about school, shared laughs over old memories, and discussed their future plans. The conversation flowed easily, and Amélie felt a sense of belonging and comfort that she had been missing.

As the afternoon wore on, Philippe suggested they visit a nearby park. The weather was improving, and the park's pathways were beginning to show signs of life. They spent some time walking and talking, enjoying the beauty of the emerging season. The experience was rejuvenating for Amélie, offering a break from her usual routine and a reminder of the support network she had in her friends.

Back at home, Amélie found herself reflecting on the day's events. She realized that while the grief of losing her grandfather was still present, there were moments of joy and connection that were equally significant. These moments were not about forgetting her loss but about finding a way to live with it and to cherish the support she received from those around her.

As spring approached, Amélie felt a growing sense of optimism. The changing seasons seemed to symbolize her own journey towards healing and acceptance. She continued to work on her research, now with a renewed sense of purpose and a commitment to maintaining balance in her life.

One day, Amélie found herself sitting on a park bench, reading a book as the sun cast a warm glow over the park. She reflected on how much she had grown over the past months. The pain of her grandfather's passing was still there, but she had learned to navigate it with resilience and grace. Her research continued to progress, and she was determined to honour his memory in a way that felt true to herself.

As she sat there, enjoying the serene environment, Amélie felt a profound sense of peace. The challenges she faced were far from over, but she was learning to approach them with a sense of hope and determination. The support of her family and friends, combined with her own inner strength, had guided her through some of the darkest times.

The park was filled with the sounds of spring—the rustling of leaves, the chirping of birds, and the distant laughter of children. Amélie took a deep breath, feeling a sense of renewal as she embraced the changing season. It was a reminder that even amidst the hardships, there was always the promise of new beginnings and the possibility of finding joy in the everyday moments.

As the sun began to set, casting a golden light over the park, Amélie felt a sense of contentment. She knew that the road ahead would still have its challenges, but she was ready to face them with courage and optimism. The journey of healing was ongoing, but with each step, she felt a little more at peace with herself and her place in the world.

Amélie's Diary

It's been a few months since Grandfather Alain passed away, and life has started to find a new rhythm. I've been trying to balance my research with moments of rest, and I think it's helping. The winter has given way to early signs of spring, and the changing season feels like a metaphor for my own journey.

I've been working hard on my project about Meniere's disease. It's a challenging task, but I find solace in the work, knowing that it's something Grandfather would have been proud of. Some days are easier than others. There are moments when I feel overwhelmed, and the weight of his absence feels heavier than usual. But then I remind myself of the progress I'm making and the goals I set for myself.

I'm learning to take breaks and find joy in small things. Alex has been a great support, and I appreciate his encouragement. We took a walk together the other day, and it was refreshing to step away from my work and just be outside. The changing weather and the signs of spring were a welcome reminder that life moves forward, even when we're feeling stuck.

Spending time with friends like Philippe and Cécile has also been a big help. We met up recently, and it was nice to talk and laugh about old memories. It's moments like those that remind me of the importance of connection and the support of those who care about me. I've realized that even though Grandfather is no longer here, his memory lives on through the love and support of those around me.

I've been trying to keep up with my studies and my research, but it's not always easy. There are days when I feel like I'm not making enough progress or when I'm frustrated with myself for not achieving more. But I'm learning to be patient and to accept that it's okay to have off days. I'm doing my best to find a balance between my work and my well-being.

I've also started taking up new hobbies to help me relax. Sketching and reading have become my go-to activities when I need a break from my research. They offer a different kind of escape and help me unwind. It's amazing how something as simple as a good book or a drawing can provide comfort and clarity.

Sometimes, I still find myself thinking about Grandfather and wishing he were here to see what I'm working on. But I also know that he would want me to keep moving forward and to make the most of the opportunities I have. I'm trying to honour his memory by staying focused on my goals and by being kind to myself along the way.

Overall, I feel like I'm slowly finding my footing again. There are still tough days, and the sadness of losing Grandfather is something I'll carry with me. But I'm also finding moments of joy and connection that remind me of the beauty in life, even amidst the challenges.

I'm looking forward to what the future holds, and I'm determined to continue working towards my goals while taking care of myself. The journey is ongoing, but I'm hopeful that with each passing day, I'll find more balance and peace.

Amélie

Chapter 19: A Winter's Reunion

The biting chill of winter lingered in the air as Amélie and Alex prepared for their family's arrival. Snow blanketed the landscape in a serene white layer, transforming their surroundings into a picturesque winter scene. Despite the cold, a warm sense of anticipation filled their home. Amélie had spent the past few days preparing for this visit, meticulously arranging every detail to create a welcoming environment for Henri, Jasmine, Léon, James, and Èlodie.

The house was adorned with seasonal decorations, and a soft glow emanated from the fireplace, casting a cozy ambiance throughout the living room. Amélie had set up a comfortable area by the fire for their guests, with plush blankets and pillows arranged to ensure everyone would be warm and relaxed. Despite the care she had taken, a knot of anxiety remained in her stomach, a reminder of the complex emotions she was navigating.

As the time for their arrival drew closer, Amélie and Alex finished their preparations. Alex, who had been diligently helping with the final touches, came over to join Amélie in the living room. "Everything looks great," he said, his smile reassuring. "I think they'll appreciate all the effort you've put in."

"I hope so," Amélie replied, her voice tinged with both excitement and nerves. "I really want everything to go well."

Their conversation was interrupted by the sound of car doors closing outside. The rumble of engines and the crunch of tires on snow signalled that their guests had arrived. Amélie and Alex exchanged a glance, and with a deep breath, they moved toward the front door to greet their family.

Henri was the first to step into the house, his tall figure wrapped in a thick winter coat. His face lit up with a broad smile as he saw Amélie and Alex. "Amélie! Alex!" he exclaimed, his voice full of warmth. He swept them both into a hearty embrace. "It's so wonderful to see you!"

"It's great to see you too, Henri," Amélie said, her smile genuine. The warmth of his hug helped ease her lingering anxiety.

Jasmine followed Henri, her demeanour more reserved but marked by a noticeable softness. "Hello, everyone," she said, her tone significantly gentler than it had been in the past. "Thank you for hosting us."

"Hello, Jasmine," Amélie replied, her smile tinged with cautious optimism. "It's nice to see you."

As the rest of the family arrived, Léon, James, and Èlodie made their way into the house. Léon gave Alex a nod of recognition before taking a seat in the living room. James approached Amélie with a friendly grin. "Hi, Amélie. How've you been?"

"I've been well, thanks," Amélie responded, shaking his hand. "It's nice to see you."

Èlodie, seemingly preoccupied, offered only a brief "Hey" before quickly returning to her compact mirror. Despite her aloofness, Amélie was determined to make the most of the visit.

Once everyone was settled inside, Henri took in the inviting atmosphere with appreciation. "This place looks fantastic, Amélie," he said, genuinely impressed. "You've done a wonderful job."

"Thank you, Henri," Amélie replied, feeling a wave of relief at his compliment.

The family's presence began to create a sense of comfort within the home. Henri and Jasmine engaged in conversations with Amélie and Alex, their interactions marked by a new sense of ease. Jasmine's approach was notably more friendly as she helped with the meal preparations and participated in light-hearted conversations.

"So, how have your studies been going, Amélie?" Jasmine asked, her tone both curious and supportive. "I've heard you've been doing amazing things."

"It's been a challenge, but I'm managing," Amélie replied modestly. "I've been focusing on several projects lately."

"That's really impressive," Jasmine said, nodding in approval. "I'm glad to hear you're doing so well."

The afternoon passed with a growing sense of camaraderie. Henri and Jasmine, along with Léon, James, and Èlodie, engaged in various conversations, catching up on family news and sharing stories. The warmth in the house was a stark contrast to the cold winter landscape outside, and it provided a much-needed comfort to Amélie.

The meal was a lively affair, filled with laughter and engaging discussions. Jasmine's newfound warmth was evident in her participation, and her interactions with Amélie were marked by a genuine effort to connect. Henri, ever the optimist, observed the positive changes with satisfaction, pleased to see the family dynamics improving.

As the evening approached, Henri gathered everyone in the living room for a toast. "To family," he said, raising his glass. "To the bonds that keep us together and the new beginnings we create."

Amélie felt a wave of contentment as she joined in the toast. The warmth of the evening, coupled with the genuine connections being rekindled, offered a much-needed sense of healing.

Following the toast, the family settled into comfortable chairs by the fire, sharing stories and reflecting on their experiences. The conversation flowed naturally, marked by moments of humour and heartfelt exchanges. Amélie, though still processing the recent challenges, found comfort in the positive interactions and the sense of unity.

As the night drew to a close, Amélie and Alex bid their relatives farewell. The visit had been a success, fostering stronger connections and mending old wounds. The shared laughter and renewed warmth were a testament to the strength of familial bonds.

The house, once again quiet, was a soothing contrast to the earlier buzz of activity. Amélie and Alex reflected on the day, feeling a renewed sense of hope and connection. The visit had provided a much-needed boost, and though the road ahead was still uncertain, they faced it with the knowledge that their family's support was a solid foundation for whatever lay ahead.

As Amélie prepared for bed that night, the echoes of the day's conversations and the warmth of the familial bonds lingered. The visit had brought a sense of renewal and a reminder of the strength of family connections. With a quiet optimism about the future, Amélie settled into bed, ready to face whatever challenges lay ahead with the support and love of her family by her side.

Amelie's diary,

Dear Diary,

Today was full of surprises. The house, usually so quiet and predictable, turned into a warm refuge in the middle of winter. Henri, Jasmine, Léon, James, and Èlodie came to visit us. To be honest, I was a little apprehensive about seeing them. So much has changed, and I didn't really know what to expect.

Jasmine, who used to be so distant and sometimes harsh with me, seemed different this time. She was much warmer, more open. Elle m'a même complimentée on how I had been handling everything since Grandpère Alain passed away. It felt strange, but in a good way. I'm not used to receiving such kindness from her, and a part of me wonders if it's genuine or if she feels guilty about something. Still, je ne peux pas m'empêcher de me sentir un peu plus légère, like a small weight has been lifted off my shoulders.

Henri was his usual kind self, always so supportive. He brought some treats and insisted that we all sit down together to enjoy them. C'était agréable, presque comme une petite fête. We shared stories, and for a moment, I could forget about all the pain and sadness that have been hanging over me these past few weeks. Mais au fond, je ne pouvais pas m'empêcher de penser à Grandpère Alain. I know he would have loved this moment, seeing us all together, trying to find joy even in the midst of winter.

Léon and James were their usual selves, full of energy and mischief. They spent most of the time teasing Alex, which made me smile. C'était bien de les voir ainsi, si insouciants, but I couldn't help but feel a bit disconnected from their carefree world. I wish I could be like them, just for a little while, without all the worries and sadness that have taken root in my heart.

Èlodie was sweet, as always. She wanted to show me her new dress, and we ended up talking about fashion for a while. Ça m'a fait du bien, just focusing on something so simple and light-hearted. Parfois, je pense que j'oublie à quel point il est important de se laisser aller à ces petits plaisirs de la vie.

But even in the midst of all these moments, I felt a deep, aching loneliness. C'est comme si une partie de moi était restée coincée dans le passé, incapable de suivre le rythme des autres. I miss Grandpère Alain so much. Il me manque tous les jours, and sometimes it feels like the pain is too much to bear. Seeing everyone together today reminded me of all the times he was with us, his laughter filling the room, his warmth wrapping around us like a blanket.

Mais aujourd'hui, j'ai appris quelque chose de nouveau. That maybe, just maybe, it's possible to start healing. Jasmine's kindness, though unexpected, was a small step. Henri's constant support, Léon and James's playful energy, and even Èlodie's innocent excitement over a dress—all of these things reminded me that life continues, even in the coldest of winters.

But still, there's a part of me that's struggling. Je me sens encore si perdue, like I'm wandering through a fog that won't lift. I keep thinking about Grandpère Alain and what he would say if he were here. Je sais qu'il me dirait to be strong, to keep moving forward, but it's hard when everything feels so overwhelming.

Peut-être que demain sera différent. Maybe I'll find more reasons to smile, more reasons to believe that things will get better. Mais pour l'instant, je prends les choses un jour à la fois. Today was a start, a small step towards something new. Et même si je ne suis pas encore prête à oublier la douleur, I think I'm ready to start finding joy again, even in the little things.

So, I'll hold on to today, to the warmth that filled the house, to the kindness I didn't expect, and to the hope that tomorrow might bring a little more light into my life.

Avec amour,

Amélie

Chapter 20: Whispers of Change

The winter days in Nice had taken on a quieter tone, the usual vibrancy of the city muted under a blanket of grey skies and the occasional drizzle. For Amélie, the chill in the air mirrored the lingering sadness in her heart. It had been several weeks since they'd returned from Québec, and while life continued to move forward, the absence of Alain was a constant presence in her thoughts.

Amélie's room, once a sanctuary of warmth and creativity, now felt like a cage. The medical journals that had once been her escape seemed almost accusatory now, their complex theories and diagrams a stark reminder of her grandfather's passing. She sat by the window, wrapped in a cozy blanket, but the comfort felt fleeting, a mere distraction from the overwhelming sense of loss.

She needed to get out. The walls of her room felt like they were closing in on her. Stepping outside, Amélie took a deep breath of the crisp winter air and walked to her favorite park. The park was quiet, save for the rustling of bare trees and the distant laughter of children. It was here, by the old wooden bench overlooking the pond, that she felt most at peace.

As she sat down, Amélie pulled out her book, but her mind kept drifting back to the hospital in Québec, to Alain's last words. "I love you and will forever be in your hearts." These words replayed in her mind, offering both comfort and an ache she couldn't quite shake.

Amélie wasn't the only one feeling the effects of the recent changes. Alex, her twin brother, had become increasingly withdrawn. Once inseparable, their bond now felt frayed, strained by the shared grief that neither of them knew how to navigate. Alex threw himself into his football practice with a fervor that bordered on obsession, but when he was home, he seemed lost in his own world, often staring out into the distance, lost in thought.

At dinner one evening, the atmosphere was heavy with unspoken words. The family gathered around the table, attempting to maintain normalcy, but the conversations were stilted, and the silence between them was palpable. Henri, ever the observer, noticed the strain and spoke up. "We've all been through a lot," he said gently. "It's okay to feel overwhelmed. We need to support each other and find a way to move forward."

Jasmine, who had been distant, now approached Amélie with an unexpected warmth. She invited Amélie to cook with her, to share evenings watching movies together. This newfound kindness was strange but welcomed. Amélie was hesitant at first but found solace in Jasmine's company. The barriers that had once seemed insurmountable began to crumble, and Amélie allowed herself to appreciate this new closeness, even if it came from a place of shared grief.

As the days continued, Amélie found herself grappling with a complex mix of emotions. She threw herself into her studies, using her medical knowledge as a distraction. She worked on designing a new surgical approach for Meniere's disease, a project she had been quietly developing. This work provided a temporary escape from her grief, a way to channel her emotions into something productive.

Her friends, Philippe and Cécile, noticed the change in her demeanour. They invited her out for coffee, hoping to offer a respite from the isolation she had been experiencing. At the café, their presence was a comfort, but Amélie struggled to fully engage in their conversation. Philippe and Cécile exchanged concerned glances but respected her need for space.

Despite her efforts to stay focused on her work and maintain a semblance of normalcy, the whispers of change were ever-present. Alex remained distant, and the family dynamics continued to shift in subtle ways. Yet, there was a growing sense that something positive might emerge from the upheaval. Henri's words about sticking together and supporting one another began to resonate more deeply with Amélie.

One evening, as the family sat around the dinner table, Henri addressed them again. "We're all dealing with this in our own way," he said. "But we're a family, and we need to remember that we have each other."

Jasmine nodded in agreement. "It's okay to feel lost, but we're here for you. All of you."

Amélie looked around at her family, noticing the small changes in their interactions. The warmth in Jasmine's eyes, the subtle encouragement from Henri, and the quiet support from Alex, even if it was unspoken. These were signs of the change that had been whispering around them, hints that things could, perhaps, begin to heal.

As the evening drew to a close, Amélie felt a flicker of hope. The grief was still there, and Alain's absence would never fully be filled, but there was love, and there was hope. And maybe, just maybe, that would be enough to start moving forward.

Amelie's Diary

Cher Journal,

It's been a few weeks since Alain passed away. I can't seem to find the right words to express what I've been feeling, and yet, here I am, writing again. Maybe because, deep down, writing has always been my way of making sense of the chaos. Of stitching together the pieces that don't seem to fit anymore.

Alain. Mon grand-père. He's gone, but I still feel him. Every day. Some days, I wake up, and it feels like the weight of the world is pressing down on my chest. I can't breathe. I can't think. Je me sens tellement perdue. I'm lost in this world without him, like a part of me has been ripped away, and I don't know how to get it back.

Everyone tells me it'll get better. They say, "Avec le temps, tu guériras." But what they don't understand is that it's not just the pain of losing Alain. It's everything. It's all the little moments I'll never have with him again. All the times I could've said something, done something, but didn't. There's so much regret, and it's suffocating.

Lately, I've been feeling strange. Different. Some days, I feel like I'm floating above everything, like nothing can touch me. I go through the motions—school, home, studying—but it all feels like a blur. Then, there are days when everything hits me all at once. I feel everything so intensely, and it's like I'm drowning in it. One moment, I'm okay, and the next, je pleure sans raison. It's like something inside me is broken, and I don't know how to fix it.

I haven't talked to anyone about it. Not really. I mean, how do you even begin to explain something like this? How do you tell the people who care about you that you feel like you're falling apart? That some days, it feels like your mind is playing tricks on you, pulling you in different directions? I don't want to worry anyone. They're all dealing with their own grief. I can't add mine on top of it.

Alex... he's been distant lately. We used to be so close, and now, it feels like there's this unspoken distance between us. I know he's hurting too, but he won't talk about it. He throws himself into football like it's the only thing keeping him grounded, and I can't blame him. We all have our ways of coping, right? But I miss him. I miss the way things used to be between us. Before everything changed.

Maman et papa, they try so hard. They want to be strong for us, but I see the cracks. I see the way Papa's eyes lose their sparkle when he thinks no one's looking. The way Maman's voice trembles ever so slightly when she talks about Alain. I hate seeing them like this. And I hate that there's nothing I can do to fix it.

Jasmine has been different too. She used to be so... I don't know... harsh? Cold? It's like ever since Alain passed, something shifted in her. She's been kinder, softer even. The other day, she invited me to cook with her. We made one of Alain's favorite dishes, and for a moment, it felt like he was there with us. But then, the moment passed, and the emptiness came rushing back.

Cooking with Jasmine was... nice, though. It surprised me. For so long, I felt like she was someone I had to be wary of, like she was always watching and judging me. But now, it feels like she's reaching out, trying to connect. Peut-être que la douleur nous change tous.

I've been thinking a lot about medicine lately. About what Alain used to say about healing, about helping others. He always believed in me, in my dreams of becoming a doctor. I can't let him down. I've been working on my project—my secret project—for Meniere's disease. It's strange, you know? In a way, it's comforting to have something to focus on, something that's mine. A way to channel all this energy, all this pain, into something that might help people one day.

But even that feels heavy sometimes. I've been carrying this secret for so long, and part of me wonders if I'm doing the right thing by keeping it to myself. Should I tell someone? Should I let them in? But then, I think about how fragile everything feels right now, how delicate the balance is. I can't afford to break that balance. Not yet.

Philippe and Cécile have been trying to cheer me up. They take me out for coffee, invite me over to study, but I can tell they're worried. They think I'm not the same. Maybe I'm not. Maybe this is who I am now—someone who's been shaped by loss, someone who's trying to find her way in a world that feels different every day.

La vérité, c'est que je me sens fatiguée. Tired of pretending everything's okay when it's not. Tired of holding it all together when inside, I feel like I'm falling apart. I know I have to keep going. I know that's what Alain would want. But sometimes, it's hard to see the point. What's the point of all this if the people you love are just going to disappear one day?

I've been thinking a lot about life and death. About how fragile everything is. One moment, someone's here, and the next, they're gone. It's terrifying. How do you live with that knowledge? How do you wake up every day knowing that at any moment, everything could change? I don't have the answers, and it scares me.

I don't know where to go from here. I don't know how to move forward. Every step feels heavy, like I'm walking through thick fog, unable to see what's ahead. Maybe that's just how life is now. Maybe this is the new normal.

Je ne sais pas. I wish I could talk to Alain one more time. Just one more conversation. There's so much I didn't get to say, so much I didn't get to ask. But he's gone, and I have to accept that.

The world keeps spinning, even when you feel like yours has stopped. People move on. They laugh, they smile, they live. And I'm trying. I really am. But it's hard.

I've been thinking about my future, about what comes next. Medicine has always been my dream, but now... I don't know. It feels different. The passion is still there, but there's a shadow hanging over it, a heaviness I can't shake. Maybe it's just the grief talking. Maybe, in time, I'll find that spark again.

But for now, I'm just trying to make it through each day. One day at a time. That's what everyone says, right? "Take it one day at a time." But what happens when even one day feels like too much?

Je suppose que tout ce que je peux faire est d'essayer. To keep going, even when it feels impossible. To hold on to the memories of Alain, to carry him with me in everything I do.

And maybe, just maybe, one day, I'll find peace in that.

- Amélie

Chapter 21: Bridging the Distance

The air was crisp, the winter winds biting at the edges of Amélie's scarf as she stood outside her house, watching the last remnants of snow melt from the rooftop. The world had changed so much in the past few months, and yet the seasons still turned, the sun still rose and fell, indifferent to the weight on her heart. Alain's absence was still fresh, like an open wound that hadn't quite healed, and Amélie wasn't sure if it ever would. But life, as it always did, continued.

School had been a constant presence in her life—a reminder that no matter how much grief twisted inside her, the world expected her to keep moving. Today, however, wasn't just another school day. It was different. Henri, Jasmine, Léon, James, and Élodié were visiting, and their arrival marked a subtle but significant change in the air.

Jasmine, once cold and distant, had become warmer over time. Her sharp edges softened, and though the loss of Alain had affected everyone, it had also brought them closer in ways that Amélie hadn't expected. The distance between them seemed to shrink, and Jasmine, who had often been so critical of Amélie, now looked at her with something close to understanding.

"Tu es prête?" Alex's voice broke into her thoughts, his breath visible in the chilly air. He had always been her anchor, even when they didn't always see eye to eye.

Amélie nodded, adjusting her scarf as she glanced at him. He had changed too, in his own way. The boy who had once teased her relentlessly now carried himself with a weight of responsibility she hadn't seen before. It was as if Alain's passing had forced them all to grow up faster than they should have.

"On y va," she said softly, the French slipping out naturally, though she didn't feel particularly French or English today. She felt...in-between.

As they walked toward the house, Amélie's thoughts drifted to the visit. Jasmine's family hadn't been around much since the funeral, and though the occasional messages and check-ins had been comforting, there was a distance that had settled between them—a gap that Amélie wasn't sure how to bridge. But today, with them coming over, it felt like an opportunity. Maybe this was a chance to rebuild what had been lost, or at least to start.

The doorbell rang as they approached, and Amélie took a deep breath, steeling herself for the inevitable awkwardness. Alex, as always, was the first to act, opening the door with a wide smile that barely masked the tension in his shoulders.

"Salut!" Jasmine greeted, her voice more enthusiastic than Amélie had expected. She was wrapped in a long, dark coat, her makeup minimal but tasteful. Behind her, Henri stood with his usual kind smile, holding Léon's hand, while James and Élodié trailed behind, both looking slightly nervous.

"Salut, tout le monde," Amélie said, her voice soft as she stepped forward to hug Jasmine. The embrace was tentative at first, but then Jasmine squeezed her tightly, and for a moment, it felt real, like they were both trying to hold on to something that had almost been lost.

"Ça fait longtemps," Jasmine said quietly as they pulled apart, her eyes searching Amélie's face.

Amélie nodded, feeling the lump in her throat rise. "Oui, beaucoup trop longtemps."

The house felt fuller than it had in weeks, the sound of conversation filling the once-quiet rooms. Henri and Alex were deep in discussion about football, their voices rising and falling with excitement. Léon and James had disappeared into the living room, where they were probably bickering over the television remote. And Amélie found herself standing in the kitchen with Jasmine, the two of them preparing tea in a silence that was both comfortable and charged with unspoken words.

"Tu vas bien?" Jasmine asked after a long pause, her voice hesitant.

Amélie glanced at her, surprised by the question. Jasmine wasn't one to ask about feelings. She wasn't one to pry. But the way she asked now—quietly, almost vulnerably—made Amélie realize that this wasn't just a casual question. Jasmine was genuinely asking.

"J'essaie," Amélie replied, her voice barely above a whisper. She focused on the teapot in front of her, her fingers trembling slightly as she poured the hot water. "C'est difficile."

Jasmine nodded, her gaze softening as she watched Amélie. "Je sais. On a tous beaucoup perdu."

For a moment, neither of them said anything. The only sound was the gentle clink of teacups being placed on the counter, and the distant laughter of Henri and Alex in the other room. But despite the quiet, there was an understanding that passed between them—a shared grief that they hadn't spoken of before.

Jasmine's warmth was something Amélie hadn't expected, and though it felt strange, it also felt like a bridge between them. The distance that had once existed—the tension, the misunderstandings—seemed to be fading. Maybe, just maybe, they were starting to find their way back to each other.

As they carried the tea into the living room, Amélie found herself smiling for the first time in what felt like ages. It wasn't a big smile—it wasn't even a particularly happy one—but it was there, and that was something.

The afternoon passed in a blur of conversation and shared memories, with Henri telling stories about Alain that made everyone laugh and cry in equal measure. Alex, for all his teasing, had a gentleness about him that surfaced in moments like these. He had a way of knowing exactly when to crack a joke and when to let the silence speak for itself.

By the time the sun began to set, casting long shadows across the floor, the tension that had lingered earlier in the day seemed to have dissipated. Jasmine was laughing, her arm casually draped over the back of the couch as she watched Henri and Alex argue over the best football teams. Léon and James were playing some game on the floor, their faces scrunched in concentration, while Élodié had fallen asleep on Amélie's lap, her small body curled up like a cat.

For a moment, everything felt...normal.

Amélie rested her head against the back of the couch, her fingers gently brushing through Élodié's hair as she stared at the ceiling. She could hear the muffled voices of her family around her, the clatter of dishes in the kitchen, the soft hum of life moving on. And for the first time in a long time, she felt at peace.

It didn't last long.

Later that night, after everyone had left and the house had returned to its usual stillness, Amélie found herself alone in her room, staring at the project she had been working on for weeks. The surgical cure for Menière's disease was spread out on her desk in a mess of notes and diagrams, her own handwriting scrawled across the pages like a map of her thoughts. It had become her obsession, her way of coping with the chaos that had consumed her life.

But now, looking at it, she felt...nothing.

The excitement that had once driven her—the determination to make something of herself, to honour Alain's memory—had been replaced by a numbness she couldn't shake. It was as if the project, which had once been her lifeline, had become just another burden.

Amélie sighed, rubbing her eyes as she pushed the papers aside. She couldn't focus. Not tonight.

Instead, she pulled out her journal, the one place where she could let her thoughts spill out without judgment. She hadn't written in it for days—maybe weeks—but tonight, she felt the urge to write. To put into words the things she couldn't say out loud.

Amélie's Diary

Dear Journal,

Today was...strange. I don't know how else to describe it. Having Jasmine and the others over felt good in a way I didn't expect. She's been so much kinder lately, and it makes me wonder if maybe—just maybe—things can change. People can change.

But it also felt overwhelming. Being around everyone, trying to pretend like everything is okay when it's not... it's exhausting. And I know they mean well. I know they're trying. But sometimes I feel like I'm being crushed under the weight of their expectations. Everyone keeps telling me I'm so strong, that I'm handling this so well, but what they don't see is how close I am to breaking.

Alain's death shattered something inside me, and I don't know how to put the pieces back together. Every time I think I'm getting better, something happens to remind me of how much I've lost. How much we've all lost.

And then there's the project. The cure for Menière's disease. It was supposed to be my way of moving forward, my way of proving to myself—and to Alain—that I could still do something meaningful. But now... I don't know. It feels like it's slipping through my fingers. Like I'm losing control of it, and I'm scared. I'm scared that if I let go of this, I'll have nothing left.

I miss Alain. Every day, I miss him. And no matter how hard I try to fill that void, it's still there, gnawing at me. I don't know what to do anymore. I don't know how to keep going.

Au Revoir,

Amélie

Chapter 22: A Test of Faith

Winter had settled in fully by the time Amélie woke up the next morning. The familiar chill in the air greeted her as she pulled the covers over her head, trying to block out the world for just a little longer. But it was no use—her thoughts raced too much to stay still. She knew today would be different, harder. Something felt off, and she couldn't shake the heaviness that weighed on her chest.

Sitting up slowly, Amélie reached for her phone on the nightstand. The screen lit up with a flurry of notifications—mostly messages from her friends, some homework reminders, and a few emails. She quickly swiped them away and stared at the blank screen, her reflection ghosted back at her. Today was the day of the charity event at school. It wasn't just any event either; it was one organized in memory of her grandfather, Alain.

The event had been Henri's idea initially, with Jasmine and others pitching in, but Amélie's teachers, especially Monsieur Lefebvre, had been the driving force behind making it happen. It was supposed to be a day where students, teachers, and parents came together to raise funds for Ménière's disease research—a cause close to Alain's heart. It should have felt meaningful and uplifting, yet Amélie felt torn, as if she were walking into something she wasn't quite ready to face.

She got out of bed reluctantly, heading to her wardrobe where her school uniform was neatly folded. Pulling it on, she caught sight of her reflection in the mirror. The familiar white blouse and grey skirt didn't feel the same as they used to. Her chestnut hair was messier than usual, her eyes duller. A part of her barely recognized the girl staring back at her.

"Amélie, hurry up, we're going to be late!" Alex's voice echoed from downstairs, breaking through her fog of thoughts. He had always been punctual—something she both appreciated and found irritating. But today, she was glad for his insistence.

"J'arrive!" Amélie called back, adjusting her tie before heading downstairs.

Alex was waiting at the bottom of the stairs, leaning against the banister. He was already dressed in his school uniform, a serious look on his face. Despite the usual teasing and sibling bickering, he'd been more attentive lately, especially since Alain had passed. Amélie could see the subtle changes in him too—the way his jokes had become softer, more careful, and how he seemed to watch over her even more.

"Ready for today?" Alex asked, his voice low as they walked out the door together, their footsteps crunching on the frosty pavement.

Amélie hesitated before nodding. "I guess so."

Alex glanced at her, concern flickering in his eyes, but he didn't push it. He knew better than anyone how fragile she could be these days, how easily she could retreat into herself. The walk to school was mostly quiet, save for the occasional burst of wind that whipped through the trees.

By the time they reached the gates, the school grounds were bustling with activity. Banners for the event were strung up between the buildings, and students milled about, setting up tables, booths, and banners. A large sign near the entrance read, *Charity Event in Memory of Alain Dubois: Supporting Ménière's Disease Research.* Seeing it sent a pang of sorrow through Amélie's chest.

"I'll catch up with you later," Alex said, giving her a quick pat on the shoulder before heading off to help set up one of the booths with his friends. Amélie lingered by the entrance, unsure of where to go.

"Amélie!" a familiar voice called out.

She turned to see Philippe and Cécile hurrying over to her, their faces bright with excitement. They both wore matching school uniforms, though Philippe had somehow managed to make his look more casual, with his tie askew and his shirt untucked. Cécile, ever the perfectionist, looked immaculate as always.

"Are you helping with the event?" Philippe asked, his voice slightly breathless from running over. "We're doing the raffle booth. Should be fun."

Amélie gave a half-smile, the kind she had perfected over the past few weeks. "I'm supposed to be helping with the bake sale, I think."

Cécile nodded sympathetically. "It must be tough, doing this for Alain. But it's such a wonderful way to honour him."

Amélie swallowed hard. Cécile meant well, but sometimes her words felt like salt in an open wound. "Yeah, I know."

Before the conversation could go any further, Monsieur Lefebvre appeared, his tall, commanding presence instantly capturing their attention. He was one of the few teachers Amélie had always admired—his calm demeanour and sharp intellect made him a favorite among students.

"Ah, Amélie," he said, his deep voice warm and reassuring. "I was hoping to catch you before things got too busy. Could I speak with you for a moment?"

Amélie nodded, feeling the familiar nervousness she always felt around him. "Of course."

Monsieur Lefebvre motioned for her to follow him, and they walked together toward one of the quieter hallways inside the school. The sound of students setting up for the event faded as they moved away from the crowd.

"Amélie, I wanted to talk to you about today," Monsieur Lefebvre began, his voice measured. "I know this event is very personal for you, and I want you to know that if at any point it becomes too much, you are under no obligation to stay. You've been through a lot, and I don't want you to feel like you have to push yourself too hard."

Amélie felt a lump form in her throat. "I want to be here. For Alain. He would have wanted this."

Monsieur Lefebvre gave her a gentle smile. "That's very noble of you, but remember that Alain would also want you to take care of yourself. It's okay to need a break, Amélie. You've been carrying a lot on your shoulders."

Amélie nodded, though she wasn't sure she fully believed him. Taking a break felt like giving up, and giving up wasn't an option.

"I'll be fine," she said, her voice more determined than she felt.

Monsieur Lefebvre studied her for a moment before nodding. "All right. Just know that we're all here for you if you need anything. And remember, it's not about being perfect. It's about doing your best."

As they walked back to the main hall, Amélie couldn't shake the feeling of unease that had settled in her chest. She wanted to believe that she could handle today, but the weight of the event, the memories of Alain, and the pressure she put on herself were starting to feel overwhelming.

The charity event was already in full swing by the time they returned. Booths lined the courtyard, and students, teachers, and parents milled about, buying baked goods, entering raffles, and donating to the cause. Amélie spotted her friends at the bake sale booth, and with a deep breath, she made her way over to join them.

The day passed in a blur of activity. Amélie helped sell cakes and pastries, exchanged polite smiles with teachers and parents, and even managed to laugh a few times at Philippe's bad jokes. But underneath it all, she felt a growing sense of detachment, as if she were watching the event unfold from a distance.

As the sun began to set and the crowd thinned out, Amélie found herself standing by the memorial booth that had been set up in Alain's honour. It was simple—just a table with photos of him and a small donation box for Ménière's disease research. Seeing his face, smiling back at her from the pictures, brought a fresh wave of grief crashing over her.

She stood there for a long time, staring at the photos, lost in thought. The memories of Alain flooded her mind—his laughter, his warmth, the way he had always believed in her, even when she didn't believe in herself. And now he was gone, and she was left to carry on without him.

"Amélie?" a soft voice interrupted her thoughts.

She turned to see Cécile standing beside her, a look of concern on her face. "Are you okay?"

Amélie nodded quickly, wiping at her eyes before any tears could fall. "Yeah, I'm fine. Just... thinking."

Cécile didn't push her, but she stayed by her side, offering a quiet comfort that Amélie appreciated more than words could express.

As the evening drew to a close and the event wound down, Amélie found herself standing in the now-empty courtyard, the cold night air biting at her skin. The weight of the day, the memories of Alain, and the pressure she had put on herself finally caught up to her. She felt exhausted, emotionally and physically drained.

Alex found her not long after, his usual confident stride slowed as he approached her. "You okay?" he asked, his voice soft.

Amélie nodded, though she wasn't sure if it was true. "Yeah. Just... tired."

Alex didn't say anything, but he wrapped his arm around her shoulders and pulled her into a hug. For a moment, they stood there in the quiet, the world around them fading away. It was just the two of them, brother and sister, trying to navigate their way through the grief and the pain together.

"You did good today," Alex said after a while, his voice muffled by her hair. "Alain would be proud."

Amélie's Diary

Dear Diary,

Today was supposed to be a day of remembrance, a day dedicated to Alain. And yet, I can't help but feel like I've failed somehow. I woke up this morning with a strange mix of emotions—nervousness, sadness, maybe even a bit of hope that today would offer some kind of closure. I thought that by contributing to something in Alain's name, it would make the grief easier to bear, that I could somehow make sense of everything that's happened. But as the day went on, the weight of it all just seemed to grow heavier.

The charity event was bustling from the moment I arrived at school. Everywhere I looked, there were students setting up booths, decorating, and preparing for the day ahead. The banners that hung from the school entrance, adorned with Alain's name, were a constant reminder of why we were all here. I should have felt pride seeing it, but instead, it only served as a painful reminder that he's really gone.

Alex was there, of course, doing his usual thing—helping with the football shootout and making sure everything was running smoothly. He's been so strong through all of this, always looking out for me, but I know he's hurting too. He doesn't say it, but I can tell. There's a certain sadness in his eyes lately, like he's trying to keep it together for my sake.

I spent most of the day at the bake sale booth, selling cakes and cookies that people had donated. Every time someone bought something, I couldn't help but wonder if they really understood what this event meant, or if it was just another school function to them. I wanted to tell everyone about Alain, about how incredible he was, about the way he would light up a room with his smile, and how much he believed in me. But I couldn't. The words got stuck in my throat every time I tried to speak.

It's hard to explain, but it felt like I was walking through the day in a haze, like I was there but not really there. People would talk to me, and I would nod and smile, but it all felt so distant, like I was watching everything happen from the outside. Even when Philippe and Cécile came over to check on me, I couldn't bring myself to engage with them the way I usually would. Philippe, in his usual goofy way, tried to cheer me up with jokes that didn't really land, and Cécile was her usual supportive self, offering me quiet words of comfort. I appreciated it, I really did, but it didn't change the fact that something inside me felt off.

As the day went on, I found myself drawn to the memorial booth we had set up for Alain. It was a simple table with photos of him and a donation box for Ménière's disease research, which was the whole point of today. Standing there, looking at those photos, everything came rushing back—the memories, the grief, the emptiness. I could almost hear his voice in my head, see him smiling at me the way he used to.

I stood there for what felt like hours, just staring at his pictures. It was like I was frozen in place, unable to move, unable to breathe. All I could think about was how much I missed him, how unfair it was that he was taken from us so soon. He was supposed to be here, cheering us on, telling us how proud he was of everything we were doing. But instead, we were left to honour him without him, and that thought hurt more than anything.

Cécile found me there, of course. She always seems to know when I need someone, even when I don't say anything. She didn't push me to talk, didn't ask how I was feeling. She just stood beside me in silence, offering her presence as a form of comfort. I'm grateful for that, for her understanding that sometimes words aren't enough.

I think the hardest part of today was realizing that no matter how much we do in Alain's memory, it will never bring him back. I know that sounds obvious, but it hit me in a way I wasn't expecting. All the fundraising, all the donations—it's important, and I know it will help others who are struggling with Ménière's disease, but it doesn't fill the void he left behind. It doesn't make the pain any less.

And then there's the guilt. The guilt of not being able to do more, of not being able to make a bigger impact. I keep thinking about how Alain always believed in me, how he always said I would do great things, and I can't help but feel like I'm letting him down. Today, I tried to do something in his name, something that would make him proud, but it just feels like it wasn't enough. I don't know if it ever will be.

As the event started winding down, I found myself standing in the courtyard, watching as people packed up and went home. The air was cold, and the sky had turned a soft shade of pink as the sun began to set. It should have been a peaceful moment, but all I could feel was this overwhelming sense of exhaustion—not just physically, but emotionally.

Alex came to find me after a while. He didn't say much, just wrapped his arm around my shoulders and gave me one of his brotherly hugs. It's funny, we don't always get along, but in moments like this, he knows exactly what I need. He told me I did a good job today, that Alain would be proud, and I wanted to believe him. I really did. But deep down, I'm not sure if I believe it myself.

The walk home was quiet, and I was grateful for that. I didn't have the energy to talk, and Alex seemed to sense that. When we got home, Mum and Dad asked how the event went, and I gave them the usual polite responses—"It was good," "People were generous," "We raised a lot of money"—but I didn't tell them how I was really feeling. I didn't tell them about the emptiness, the guilt, the sense of failure that's been hanging over me all day. I don't think they'd understand.

Now, sitting here in my room, with the house quiet and dark, I feel like I can finally breathe. But even that's hard. The weight of today is still pressing down on me, and I don't know how to shake it off. I thought that by doing something for Alain, by honouring him in this way, it would make the grief easier to bear. But it hasn't. If anything, it's made me realize just how deep that grief runs, how much I'm still struggling to come to terms with everything.

I miss him, Diary. I miss him so much. And I'm scared that this feeling, this emptiness, is never going to go away. I keep telling myself that it will get better with time, that eventually, I'll find a way to move forward, but right now, it feels impossible.

There's a part of me that wants to believe what everyone keeps telling me—that Alain would be proud, that I'm doing enough, that I'm not letting him down. But there's another part of me that's filled with doubt, with fear that I'll never be able to live up to his expectations, that I'll never be able to make him as proud as he always thought I would.

I don't know what's next. I don't know how to move forward from here. But I guess that's part of life, isn't it? Figuring it out as you go, even when you don't have all the answers.

Maybe tomorrow will be better. Maybe tomorrow, I'll find a little more strength, a little more clarity. But for now, I just need to rest. I need to let go of today, even if just for a moment.

Goodnight, Diary.

Amélie

Chapter 23: A New Dawn

The morning light streamed through the window as Amélie opened her eyes. For the first time in what felt like months, the weight on her chest felt lighter. There was still sorrow, yes, but it no longer consumed her. It was as though the grief had found a place within her, not taking over, but existing quietly alongside everything else.

Sitting up, Amélie glanced at her desk, where scattered papers, notes, and scribbles lay in a chaotic heap. Among the mess was something that had kept her mind occupied, something that brought her back to life in a way she hadn't expected. The equation she had been working on for weeks, an idea that had sparked from her own deep interest in surgery and Alain's memory. This equation had the potential to revolutionise the way surgeons approached their work—how they could predict the outcome of a surgery and adjust their plan accordingly. It was her way of contributing to the medical field she had always dreamed of being part of, and it was also her way of honouring her brother's belief in her genius.

She spent days refining the equation, checking every variable, every factor, making sure it could stand up to scrutiny. It wasn't just about performing surgery; it was about helping surgeons make decisions in real-time, adapting their approach mid-surgery to ensure the best possible outcomes. It was a tool that could save lives, and she was eager to share it with the world—or at least with her teachers first.

Amélie had always known her science teachers, Madame Laramie and Docteur Michel, were supportive, but recently, they had been especially kind. They had both known about her struggles with losing Alain, and rather than pressure her to meet deadlines or push her too hard, they had given her the space to heal. Yet, they also reminded her, gently, of her own potential, the potential Alain had always seen in her. Today, she would finally show them her work.

At breakfast, Alex sat across from her, glancing at her over his cereal. He seemed calmer too, after weeks of tension and grief. They hadn't talked much in recent days, but there was an unspoken understanding between them—both siblings were slowly healing, in their own ways.

"You've been up late working on that thing, haven't you?" Alex said, eyeing the papers poking out of her schoolbag.

Amélie nodded, a slight smile on her face. "It's nearly done. I'm showing Madame Laramie and Docteur Michel today."

Alex raised his eyebrows in approval. "You've always been good at that stuff. They'll be impressed."

The rest of the morning passed in a blur as Amélie prepared herself for school. She tucked the final draft of her equation into a folder, feeling a mix of excitement and nerves. There was a sense of purpose driving her now, something she hadn't felt in a long time.

At school, she found herself standing outside the science block, where Madame Laramie and Docteur Michel's offices were. It was quiet, and for a moment, Amélie hesitated, wondering if she should even bother them with something that, in her mind, still needed more refining. But then she thought of Alain and how he'd always pushed her to go further, to trust in her abilities.

Stepping inside, she found Madame Laramie at her desk, scribbling notes in a textbook. The teacher looked up and smiled warmly when she saw Amélie.

"Amélie! I've been meaning to talk to you. How are you feeling?" Madame Laramie asked, her voice full of genuine concern.

Amélie shifted her weight awkwardly. "Better. A lot better, actually."

Madame Laramie nodded, as if she had expected this. "I'm glad to hear it. I know it hasn't been easy, but you've shown incredible strength."

Just then, Docteur Michel entered the room, her sharp eyes immediately noticing the folder in Amélie's hand. "What have you got there, Amélie?" she asked with curiosity.

Amélie hesitated for a second before handing the folder to her. "It's something I've been working on. It's an equation—well, more like a model—for surgery. It's designed to help surgeons predict the outcome of a procedure and adjust the plan during surgery, based on real-time data. I thought... I thought it could help make surgeries more efficient and safer."

Docteur Michel's expression shifted from curiosity to deep interest. She flipped through the pages, her eyes scanning the intricate calculations and formulas Amélie had meticulously developed. Madame Laramie moved closer, peering over her shoulder.

"This is incredible, Amélie," Madame Laramie said, her voice tinged with awe. "You've taken something so complex and made it... accessible. It's like you've given surgeons a roadmap to navigate even the most difficult procedures."

Docteur Michel nodded in agreement, her analytical mind already working through the implications. "If this works the way you've designed it, it could be a game-changer for the medical field. Surgeons often have to make quick decisions based on limited information. Your model could help them make more informed choices, potentially saving lives."

Hearing those words, Amélie's heart swelled with pride. This was the validation she had been seeking, the proof that her work mattered, that she could make a difference.

"It's not just about predicting the outcome," Amélie added, her confidence growing. "It's about giving surgeons the ability to adapt in real time, to see where things are headed before it's too late to make changes."

Madame Laramie smiled. "You've always had a way of thinking beyond the immediate problem. That's what makes you special, Amélie."

Amélie felt a warmth spread through her at the compliment. It had been so long since she'd allowed herself to feel proud of her abilities. The grief had overshadowed everything, but now, there was a sense of light breaking through.

Docteur Michel placed the folder on the desk and looked at Amélie thoughtfully. "You've been through so much recently, and yet you've created something extraordinary. But I want you to remember one thing, Amélie: balance. You're a brilliant student, and your work is exceptional, but you also need to take care of yourself. Don't let this drive for perfection consume you. You're still healing, and it's okay to take things slowly."

Amélie nodded, absorbing her teacher's words. "I know. I'm trying to find that balance. It's just hard sometimes."

"It will get easier," Madame Laramie said gently. "And we'll be here to support you through it."

The rest of the conversation was filled with technical discussions about the equation, with both teachers offering insights and suggestions to refine it further. But underlying it all was their unwavering support, not just for Amélie's academic endeavours, but for her well-being as a whole. They understood that she wasn't just a student, but a young girl navigating grief, genius, and the complexities of growing up.

As the day ended and Amélie made her way home, there was a newfound lightness in her step. The sorrow hadn't disappeared entirely, but it no longer held her captive. She had something to look forward to, something that gave her purpose and direction.

And as she sat at her desk that evening, reviewing the notes from her meeting with Madame Laramie and Docteur Michel, she felt a quiet sense of satisfaction. This equation, this model—it wasn't just numbers on a page. It was a piece of her, a way to make the world a little better, a way to honour Alain's memory by continuing to push forward, even when it seemed impossible.

Amélie's Diary

Dear Diary,

It's strange, isn't it? How one moment you feel like the whole world is crumbling around you, and the next, there's this small glimmer of hope that pulls you through. Today was one of those days. For the first time in so long, I didn't feel trapped under the weight of everything that's happened. The sadness is still there, of course. I don't think that ever truly goes away. But it's like it's moved to a corner of my heart instead of taking over all of it.

I showed Madame Laramie and Docteur Michel my equation today. I've been working on it for weeks, but I've kept it hidden from everyone, even Alex. I wasn't sure if it was ready or if I was ready to share it. But today... I just felt like I had to. It's funny how something like this, just a series of numbers and calculations, could become so important to me. It's not just an equation—it's a way to bring order to the chaos, a way to feel like I can still make a difference in the world despite everything that's been going on.

When I handed them the folder, I was terrified. What if it wasn't good enough? What if they thought it was silly? But their reaction... oh, Diary, I've never felt so proud. Docteur Michel said it could revolutionize surgery, that it could help surgeons make better decisions in real-time. Hearing that from her, from someone I admire so much, it made me feel like maybe I'm not just a kid after all. Maybe I really can do something meaningful, something that will matter.

But it wasn't just the validation that meant so much to me. It was the way they talked to me—not just about my work, but about me. They could see how hard I've been struggling, even though I haven't said much about it. Docteur Michel told me I need to find balance, that I shouldn't let the drive for perfection consume me. She's right. I know she's right. But it's so hard sometimes. It's like I have to prove something, not just to them, but to myself. Maybe even to Alain.

Alain... God, I miss him so much. Every day. It's like there's this gaping hole in my life where he used to be. I wonder if he'd be proud of me if he saw what I've been working on. I hope he would be. I hope he knows that everything I'm doing now, all the work, the equations, it's all because of him. He was the one who always pushed me to go further, to trust in my own abilities. I wish he were here to see it.

Alex has been quieter lately, but I think he's starting to feel a little better too. We don't talk much about Alain anymore. I think it's too hard for both of us, but there's this silent understanding between us. We're both hurting, but we're also both trying to heal in our own ways. He's been supportive in his own way, though. When I told him about the equation this morning, he didn't say much, but the look in his eyes... I think he's proud of me, too.

Sometimes I wonder if I'm pushing myself too hard. I can feel the exhaustion creeping in, both mentally and physically. But I can't stop, Diary. I don't know how to. There's this constant drive inside me, this need to keep going, to keep proving that I can be something more than just the girl who lost her brother.

I wish I could find that balance Docteur Michel was talking about. I wish I could just... breathe. But every time I try to relax, I feel this overwhelming sense of guilt, like I'm wasting time, like I should be doing something more. It's exhausting, and sometimes I feel like I'm drowning in my own expectations.

But today gave me hope. Just a little, but it's there. Maybe things won't always be this hard. Maybe there's a way to keep moving forward without losing myself in the process. Madame Laramie and Docteur Michel believe in me, and that means the world to me. They've been so supportive, not just as teachers, but as people who understand what it's like to go through tough times. They've given me the space I need, but they've also gently pushed me to keep going, to keep believing in myself. I'm grateful for them, more than they'll ever know.

I wonder where this will all lead. The equation, the research, the healing. It feels like the start of something, though I'm not entirely sure what yet. Maybe I'll never know for sure, but for now, I'm okay with that. I'm learning to be okay with not having all the answers.

I miss Alain, but today, for the first time, I felt like I could miss him without falling apart. That's progress, isn't it? I hope it is.

For now, I'll keep working. I'll keep trying. And I'll keep hoping that, eventually, things will get easier.

Until tomorrow, Diary.

Amélie

Chapter 24: Le Soir de Parents

The crisp winter air nipped at the faces of students and parents alike as they entered the school building for Le Soir de Parents. The evening had been marked on the school calendar for weeks, a chance for teachers to discuss the progress and challenges of their students with their families. For Amélie and Alex, it was a moment both anticipated and dreaded, an opportunity to understand their academic journey in a more personal context.

As Amélie and Alex walked into the school lobby, the familiar sight of their classmates' parents milling about made the atmosphere buzz with a mix of excitement and nervous energy. The hallways were decorated with colourful student artwork and science projects, evidence of the hard work and creativity that filled their school.

Madame Laramie, Monsieur Lefebvre, and Docteur Michel stood by the entrance, greeting parents with warm smiles. Amélie couldn't help but notice how Madame Laramie's eyes seemed to light up when she saw her. The warmth and encouragement from her science teacher were something Amélie deeply valued, especially after the recent struggles she had faced.

Monsieur Lefebvre, with his ever-present charm, was engaged in animated conversation with a group of parents, while Docteur Michel, always the embodiment of grace under pressure, was speaking quietly with a parent whose child had recently faced academic challenges.

As Amélie and Alex approached the group, Madame Laramie was the first to spot them. Her face softened into a genuine smile.

"Amélie, Alex, I'm so glad you could make it," she said, her voice kind and reassuring.

"Thank you, Madame Laramie," Amélie replied, feeling a tinge of nerves as she glanced at Alex. He seemed just as apprehensive, his usual confident demeanour replaced by a quiet anxiety.

Monsieur Lefebvre nodded in acknowledgment. “Bonsoir, Amélie, Alex. I’ve been looking forward to discussing your progress.”

“Bonsoir,” Amélie and Alex chorused, their voices echoing slightly in the spacious hallway.

Docteur Michel stepped forward, her expression warm and encouraging. “It’s good to see you both here. I’ve heard so much about your recent work, Amélie.”

Amélie blushed slightly. “Thank you, Docteur Michel. I’ve been working on a new project. I hope it’s been going well.”

“Your dedication is evident,” Docteur Michel assured her. “I’m looking forward to our discussion.”

The group moved toward the classrooms where individual meetings were scheduled. Amélie felt a flutter of nervousness in her stomach as they approached the first classroom. The walls were lined with student reports, and each desk was occupied by a parent or guardian discussing their child’s academic progress with a teacher.

Madame Laramie ushered Amélie and Alex to a quiet corner where she began to speak about their academic achievements and areas for improvement. Her tone was supportive and constructive, and Amélie felt a sense of relief wash over her as Madame Laramie praised her recent work, especially the progress she’d made with her scientific projects.

“Amélie,” Madame Laramie began, “your project on surgical equations has been exceptional. It’s clear that you’ve put a lot of effort into it, and I think it has real potential.”

Amélie’s face lit up with pride. “Thank you, Madame Laramie. I’ve been working hard on it.”

Monsieur Lefebvre, who was discussing Alex’s performance with him, glanced over and added, “Alex has shown great improvement in his recent projects. His dedication is commendable.”

Alex nodded, though he was visibly tense. “Thanks, Monsieur Lefebvre. I’ve been trying to keep up with everything.”

As the discussions continued, Amélie couldn't help but notice the supportive dynamic between her teachers and her family. Madame Laramie and Docteur Michel were genuinely interested in her progress, not just as a student but as a person. They understood the personal challenges she had been facing and offered words of encouragement and advice.

When it was time for Amélie's one-on-one with Docteur Michel, she felt a sense of reassurance. The science teacher had been a beacon of support through her recent struggles, and her kind words had always been a source of comfort.

"Amélie," Docteur Michel said softly, "I want you to know how much I admire your resilience. It's not just about your academic achievements; it's about how you've managed to keep moving forward despite everything."

Amélie looked down, her cheeks flushing with gratitude. "It's been tough, but I've had a lot of support."

"Remember, it's okay to take a step back when you need to," Docteur Michel continued. "Balancing your work with your well-being is crucial. We're all here to support you."

As the evening progressed, Amélie and Alex spoke with their parents about their experiences and future goals. The discussions were filled with encouragement and a few heartfelt moments of reflection. It was clear that, despite the challenges they had faced, the support from their teachers and family was unwavering.

Leaving the school that evening, Amélie felt a renewed sense of hope. The conversations with her teachers had given her valuable insights and reaffirmed her belief in her own abilities. It was a step toward rebuilding her confidence and finding balance in her life.

As she walked beside Alex, she glanced at him and said, "I think tonight was really helpful. It's nice to know that we're not alone in this."

Alex nodded, his expression softening. "Yeah, I agree. It feels good to have that support."

They walked in silence for a moment, the cold air invigorating them as they made their way home. The evening had been a reminder that, despite the struggles and the sorrow, there was a path forward. The support from their teachers, the encouragement from their parents, and the strength they found in each other were all steps toward a brighter tomorrow.

Amélie knew that the road ahead would still have its challenges, but she felt more prepared to face them. Le Soir de Parents had been more than just a meeting; it had been a moment of reflection and reassurance, a reminder that they were all moving forward, one step at a time.

As they reached home, Amélie took a deep breath and felt a flicker of optimism for the first time in a while. There was a sense of peace in knowing that, with the support of those around her, she could continue to take steps toward a better future.

Amélie's Diary

Dear Diary,

The evening of Le Soir de Parents was a whirlwind of emotions, but it was also incredibly enlightening. I was a bundle of nerves as we entered the school, but the support and encouragement from my teachers and my family made everything feel a bit more manageable.

Madame Laramie greeted us with such warmth, and it was comforting to hear her praise my work on the surgical equations. It feels like such a huge part of my life right now, and having her recognize my efforts was truly uplifting. I've been working so hard on this project, hoping it could make a real difference, and her approval means more to me than I can express.

Monsieur Lefebvre was just as supportive. It's always good to hear positive feedback about Alex's progress, too. I know he's been under a lot of stress, and it's nice to see that his hard work is being noticed. Even though he was a bit tense, I could tell that he appreciated the acknowledgment.

Docteur Michel's words were like a balm to my soul. She spoke to me about balancing my work with my well-being, and it really resonated with me. Sometimes I feel like I'm on a tightrope, trying to keep everything in balance. It's reassuring to hear that it's okay to step back when I need to and that I don't have to face everything alone.

As I walked home with Alex, I felt a sense of calm that I hadn't felt in a while. The support from our teachers and the conversations we had were so helpful. It's nice to know that they see us not just as students, but as individuals who are navigating a lot of challenges.

Tonight, I'm reflecting on the evening, and while there's still some sorrow from everything we've been through, I feel hopeful. The journey ahead might still be difficult, but having this support system gives me strength. I know now that it's okay to lean on others and that I'm not alone in this.

The road to healing and progress is long, but tonight reminded me that every step forward is a victory. I'm grateful for the encouragement, the understanding, and the belief that my teachers and family have shown me.

I'm taking tonight to recharge and reflect. Tomorrow is a new day, and I'm ready to face it with renewed hope and determination.

With gratitude and hope,

Amélie

Chapter 25: Stronger Together

The early morning sun crept through the curtains of Amélie's room, casting a warm, golden glow across the room. It was a new day, and though the chill of winter still lingered in the air, there was a sense of renewal that seemed to permeate the house. Amélie woke up feeling a bit more optimistic than she had in the past few weeks. The parent-teacher evening had brought her a sense of closure and hope that she hadn't realized she needed.

Downstairs, the kitchen was bustling with activity. Alex was already at the table, flipping through his homework and sipping on his orange juice. Their parents, François and Isabelle, were preparing breakfast, a small but comforting routine that seemed to ground the family in the midst of their ongoing struggles.

"Good morning," Amélie said as she joined them at the table, her voice carrying a mix of enthusiasm and fatigue. She noticed how their faces lit up when they saw her smile, and it made her feel a bit lighter inside.

"Morning, Amélie," her mother replied warmly. "How did you sleep?"

"Better," Amélie said, nodding. "I've been thinking a lot about everything we discussed last night. I feel like I'm ready to tackle some new challenges."

François looked at her with a supportive smile. "That's the spirit. We're all here for you. Whatever you need, just ask."

Amélie's mood lifted even further at her father's words. It was this kind of support that helped her see the positive aspects of her situation, even when things felt overwhelming.

After breakfast, Amélie and Alex headed to school, walking side by side in the crisp morning air. They talked about their plans for the day, and Amélie found herself laughing more than she had in weeks. It felt good to share moments of normalcy with her brother.

At school, the day passed in a blur of activity. Amélie had a meeting with Madame Laramie and Docteur Michel to discuss her recent progress and the impact of her new surgical equation. Both of her teachers were impressed with her dedication and the potential of her work.

"You've made incredible strides, Amélie," Madame Laramie said, her eyes twinkling with pride. "Your equation could really make a difference in the medical field. I'm excited to see where you take this."

Docteur Michel nodded in agreement. "Your hard work and innovation are truly inspiring. Remember to take care of yourself as well. Balancing your ambitions with your well-being is crucial."

Amélie appreciated their words of encouragement. It was these moments of affirmation that helped her feel grounded and reminded her why she was putting so much effort into her work.

The school day ended with a sense of anticipation. Amélie was eager to get home and share her progress with her family. As she walked through the door, she was greeted by a warm hug from her mother and a smile from Alex.

"Hey, how was your day?" Alex asked, his eyes filled with curiosity.

"It was good," Amélie replied, her voice brimming with excitement. "I had a meeting with Madame Laramie and Docteur Michel. They were really supportive and think my equation could have a big impact on surgery."

"That's awesome!" Alex said, his face lighting up. "I knew you'd do great."

Their parents were waiting for them in the living room, and as they settled in, Amélie shared the details of her meeting. François and Isabelle listened attentively, offering their support and encouragement.

As the evening approached, the family gathered around the dinner table, enjoying a meal together. It was a small but meaningful moment of connection. They talked about their days, shared stories, and laughed together. It was these moments of togetherness that made everything feel a bit more manageable.

After dinner, Amélie found herself reflecting on the day's events. Despite the challenges she had faced and the lingering sadness from losing her grandfather, she felt a renewed sense of purpose. Her family's unwavering support and the encouragement from her teachers had helped her regain her confidence.

Later that evening, as she sat alone in her room, Amélie took a deep breath and looked around at the things she had accomplished. The surgical equation she had worked so hard on was a testament to her resilience and dedication. She felt a sense of pride and determination to continue pushing forward.

The phone rang, interrupting her thoughts. It was a video call from Henri, Jasmine, Léon, James, and Èlodie. They were reaching out to offer their support and check in on her. Despite the distance, their presence and kindness were a reminder that she was not alone in her journey.

As she spoke with them, Amélie felt a renewed sense of connection and strength. The support from her extended family, combined with the encouragement of her immediate family and teachers, made her feel like she was surrounded by a network of people who genuinely cared for her.

The conversation ended on a positive note, with Amélie feeling reassured and supported. She knew that while the road ahead might still be challenging, she had the strength and resilience to face it.

As she prepared for bed, Amélie took a moment to reflect on the progress she had made. Despite the sorrow and difficulties she had faced, she felt a sense of hope and determination. The love and support from her family, friends, and teachers had helped her find her way through the darkness.

With a final glance at her equation and a sense of resolve, Amélie closed her eyes and drifted off to sleep, ready to face whatever the next day had in store.

—-

This chapter highlights Amélie's journey towards healing and growth, underscoring the importance of support and resilience in overcoming challenges.

Amélie's Diary

Dear Diary,

Today was one of those days where the weight of everything that's happened seemed to lift just a little bit. The morning was bright, and the sun streaming through my window made everything feel a bit warmer. I woke up feeling more hopeful than I have in a while, and that's a nice change.

Breakfast was a comforting routine with Mum, Dad, and Alex. It felt good to sit around the table together and just be a family, even if it's a bit quieter than it used to be. Dad's words of encouragement were really touching. It's moments like these that remind me how lucky I am to have such a supportive family.

Alex and I walked to school together, and it was nice to chat and laugh about the little things. It's amazing how much a simple conversation can brighten your day. School was busy, but I had a meeting with Madame Laramie and Docteur Michel, which went really well. They were both so supportive and excited about my new surgical equation. It felt great to be validated and to know that my hard work might actually make a difference.

I'm trying hard to stay focused and motivated, even though I still have moments where I feel overwhelmed. It's been tough dealing with everything since Grand-père Alain passed away. The sadness lingers, but it's comforting to know that I have people around me who care and believe in me.

At home, I shared the news about my meeting with Mum, Dad, and Alex. They were all so proud, and it made me feel really good. We had a lovely dinner together, and it was one of those rare evenings where everything just felt right.

I had a video call with Henri, Jasmine, Léon, James, and Èlodie. It was nice to hear from them and to know that they're thinking of me.

Despite the distance, their support is a reminder that I'm not alone in this journey.

As I sit here in my room, I'm reflecting on the progress I've made and the people who have helped me get here. There's still a lot of work to do, but I'm feeling more hopeful and determined. The support from my family, friends, and teachers means everything to me. It gives me the strength to keep pushing forward, even on the tough days.

I'm ready to face whatever comes next. I know it won't always be easy, but I believe that I have the strength to get through it.

Until next time,

Amélie

Chapter 26: Amélie's Resolve

In the weeks following the family gathering and the emotional video call with Henri, Jasmine, Léon, James, and Èlodie, Amélie had found herself enveloped in a sense of renewed purpose. The fresh determination to continue her work, coupled with the growing excitement about her innovative surgical equation, had become a beacon of light in the midst of her ongoing grief. The days were still filled with a sense of melancholy, but Amélie was channelling her energy into her passion for medicine, specifically her favorite specialty: ENT (Ear, Nose, and Throat).

It was a crisp morning in late February when Amélie prepared for one of the most important meetings of her young life. The sun was just beginning to rise, casting a soft golden glow over the frost-covered streets. Amélie, Docteur Michel and Madame Laramie were dressed in their usual smart attire, feeling a mixture of nervous excitement as she checked her reflection in the mirror. Today, she was scheduled to meet with Dr. Luc Martin, a renowned ENT surgeon who had agreed to speak with her about shadowing opportunities.

Amélie had spent weeks preparing for this meeting. She had read up on Dr. Martin's work, familiarized herself with his notable surgeries, and compiled a list of insightful questions. The research was exhausting but invigorating. She was eager to showcase her knowledge and passion for the specialty that had captivated her for years.

The meeting was set to take place at a prestigious hospital located in the heart of Paris. Amélie and her science teachers arrived at the hospital with a mix of anticipation and apprehension. The building stood tall and imposing, a testament to the years of knowledge and expertise housed within its walls. Amélie's heart raced as she walked through the revolving doors, her footsteps echoing in the grand lobby.

She was directed to Dr. Martin's office, a spacious room adorned with medical journals, anatomical models, and framed certificates. Dr.

Martin himself was a distinguished-looking man with kind eyes and a warm smile. He greeted Amélie with a firm handshake and invited her to sit.

"Salut, Amélie. Sympa vous recontrer Dr. Martin said, his voice carrying a note of genuine interest.

"Bonjour, Dr. Martin. Thank you so much for taking the time to meet with me," Amélie replied, her voice steady despite her nerves.

Dr. Martin gestured for Amélie to take a seat across from his desk. "I've read about your innovative surgical equation. It's quite impressive for someone your age. What inspired you to focus on ENT?"

Amélie's face lit up with enthusiasm. "I've always been fascinated by how intricate the human body is, particularly the ENT system. I've had some personal experiences that made me more interested in this field. My grandfather had hearing issues, and I saw how important it was for him to get the right treatment. I want to make a difference in this area, and I believe that my equation could help improve surgical outcomes."

Madame Laramie, without a second thought mentioned, "She is truly amazing for her age. Considering what she knows and her expertise, Docteur Michel and I really admire all her work."

Dr. Martin listened intently, nodding appreciatively. "Your passion is evident, and your background is impressive. Have you had any practical experience in the field?"

Amélie took a deep breath. "I haven't had the opportunity to gain hands-on experience yet, but I'm eager to learn. I'd be thrilled if I could shadow you or another ENT specialist to gain more insight."

Dr. Martin leaned back in his chair, considering Amélie's request. "Shadowing opportunities are crucial for aspiring surgeons. I can see that you're dedicated for a 13-year-old and have a clear understanding of the field. I'd like to offer you a chance to shadow our ENT team here. It will give you the exposure you need and help you apply your knowledge in a real-world setting."

Amélie's heart soared with excitement. "That would be incredible! Thank you so much, Dr. Martin."

"We'll start with a few observation sessions," Dr. Martin continued. "This will allow you to get a feel for the day-to-day responsibilities of an ENT surgeon. I'm confident you'll find it both challenging and rewarding."

The meeting concluded with Dr. Martin outlining the details of the shadowing program. Amélie left the office feeling elated and grateful. She was one step closer to her goal, and the opportunity to shadow a respected surgeon like Dr. Martin was a dream come true.

As she walked back through the hospital lobby, Amélie reflected on the journey that had brought her here. The loss of her grandfather, the struggles she had faced, and the support of her family and friends had all contributed to her growth. She felt a renewed sense of purpose and was ready to embrace the challenges ahead.

The following weeks were a whirlwind of activity as Amélie began her shadowing experience. Each day brought new learning opportunities and insights into the world of ENT surgery. She observed a variety of procedures, from routine check-ups to complex surgeries, and gained a deeper understanding of the intricacies involved.

One of the most memorable experiences was witnessing a delicate ear surgery performed by Dr. Martin. The precision and skill required were awe-inspiring, and Amélie felt a deep sense of admiration for the surgeon's expertise. She took detailed notes, asked questions, and absorbed every detail with enthusiasm.

Throughout her shadowing experience, Amélie was struck by the camaraderie and dedication of the ENT team. They worked seamlessly together, each member contributing their skills and knowledge to provide the best possible care for their patients. Amélie realized that the field of ENT was not only about technical skills but also about compassion and teamwork.

In addition to the technical aspects of surgery, Amélie also had the opportunity to engage with patients. She observed how the team communicated with patients and their families, providing reassurance and answering questions. It was a valuable lesson in the importance of empathy and clear communication in healthcare.

As Amélie continued her shadowing experience, she began to feel more confident in her abilities and more determined to pursue a career in ENT surgery. She was grateful for the opportunity to learn from Dr. Martin and the ENT team and was excited about the future possibilities.

One evening, as Amélie was reflecting on her experiences, she received a message from Dr. Martin. He praised her dedication and progress and expressed his support for her continued growth. The message was a source of encouragement and further fuelled Amélie's resolve.

With each passing day, Amélie's passion for ENT surgery grew stronger. She continued to work on her surgical equation, refining it based on her observations and feedback from Dr. Martin. The equation had the potential to revolutionize surgical planning and improve patient outcomes, and Amélie was determined to see it through.

Her shadowing experience had not only deepened her understanding of ENT surgery but also reinforced her commitment to making a difference in the field. Amélie felt a renewed sense of purpose and was excited about the future.

As she looked ahead, Amélie knew that there would be challenges and obstacles along the way, but she was ready to face them with determination and resilience. The support of her family, friends, and mentors had been instrumental in her journey, and she was grateful for their encouragement.

With a heart full of hope and a mind focused on her goals, Amélie embraced the next chapter of her journey with confidence. She knew that the road ahead would be demanding, but she was prepared to meet the challenges head-on and continue working towards her dreams.

Amélie's journey was a testament to her strength and resolve. Despite the difficulties she had faced, she had remained steadfast in her pursuit of her goals. The shadowing experience had been a pivotal moment in her journey, providing her with valuable insights and reinforcing her commitment to the field of ENT surgery.

As she continued to work on her surgical equation and pursue her dreams, Amélie remained focused on her vision of making a difference in the world of medicine. She knew that the path ahead would be challenging, but she was confident in her abilities and determined to achieve her goals.

With each step she took, Amélie felt a sense of accomplishment and pride. She had overcome significant obstacles and had grown stronger as a result. Her journey reflected her resilience and determination, and she was ready to face whatever challenges lay ahead with courage and conviction.

In the end, Amélie's resolve was a testament to her strength and perseverance. She had faced adversity with grace and had emerged stronger on the other side. Her journey was far from over, but she was ready to continue pursuing her dreams with unwavering determination.

The future held endless possibilities for Amélie, and she was excited to embrace whatever came next. With a heart full of hope and a mind focused on her goals, she was prepared to make a difference in the world of medicine and beyond.

Amélie's journey was a reminder that even in the face of adversity, strength and resilience can lead to remarkable achievements. Her resolve to continue pursuing her dreams and making a difference in the world of ENT surgery was a testament to her unwavering dedication and passion. As she looked ahead, Amélie was ready to embrace the challenges and opportunities that lay before her with confidence and determination.

Amélie's Diary

Dear Diary,

It's been a whirlwind of emotions and experiences lately. Even though there are still moments when the weight of my grandfather's loss feels heavy, I'm finding solace and strength in my passion for medicine. The shadowing experience with Dr. Martin has been incredible, and it's given me a new perspective on my goals.

I feel so fortunate to have had the opportunity to observe some amazing surgeries and learn from such a skilled team. Every day in the operating room has been both inspiring and challenging. I've been able to see firsthand how intricate and delicate ENT surgeries can be. The precision required, the teamwork, and the way each member of the team contributes to the patient's care—it's all been eye-opening.

I've also been working hard on refining my surgical equation. It's something I'm really passionate about, and I believe it could make a significant difference in surgical outcomes. The feedback from Dr. Martin and the ENT team has been invaluable. I'm constantly tweaking and improving the equation based on their insights. It's a lot of work, but I'm excited about the potential impact it could have.

One of the highlights of this experience was witnessing a complex ear surgery. The skill and expertise involved were awe-inspiring, and I felt so grateful to be a part of it, even as an observer. It reaffirmed my desire to pursue a career in ENT and solidified my commitment to this field.

Despite the busy schedule and the challenges, I've found moments of joy and fulfilment in the work I'm doing. The support I've received from Dr. Martin, Madame Laramie, Monsieur Lefebvre and Docteur Michel has been incredible. They've all been so encouraging and supportive, not just in my professional journey but also in dealing with the personal struggles I've faced.

It's a strange feeling—navigating the grief of losing my grandfather while also experiencing such excitement and hope for the future. There are days when I feel a bit overwhelmed, but I'm learning to balance my emotions and stay focused on my goals. I know that my grandfather would be proud of what I'm doing, and that thought keeps me going.

I'm also really excited about the future. There's so much potential and so many possibilities. I'm looking forward to continuing my work on the surgical equation and seeing where it leads. I'm eager to dive deeper into the world of ENT and make a meaningful contribution to the field.

As I move forward, I'm reminded of the importance of perseverance and resilience. It's not always easy, but I'm committed to pushing through the challenges and staying true to my passions.

Thank you for listening, Diary. Your pages have been a safe space for me to express my thoughts and feelings. I'm grateful for this outlet and for the opportunity to reflect on my journey.

Until next time,

Amélie

Chapter 27: The Turnaround

Amélie could feel the excitement buzzing through her entire body as she walked through the hospital corridors. The winter chill outside was sharp, but inside, the energy was warm and full of life. The ENT department was a space where her love for medicine felt most alive, and every visit here only strengthened her resolve to one day become a surgeon. Her footsteps echoed as she made her way toward the operating rooms, her mind whirring with thoughts of what she might see today.

Since starting her shadowing sessions, Amélie had experienced a world of knowledge that she had only dreamed about before. She watched as surgeons performed intricate procedures, their hands steady and their concentration unwavering. Every day brought new challenges, and every day Amélie learned something new that she knew would one day be useful in her own journey. But today felt different.

She entered the observation room, where her mentor, Dr. Martin, was preparing for another complex surgery. This time, it was for a patient with advanced Meniere's disease—a condition that affected the inner ear, causing vertigo, tinnitus, and hearing loss. The surgery was delicate, requiring the utmost precision, and Amélie couldn't wait to watch Dr. Martin in action again.

"Ah, Amélie! You're just in time," Dr. Martin greeted her warmly, her eyes crinkling with a smile behind her surgical mask. "We're about to begin."

Amélie nodded eagerly, her gaze locked on the surgical team as they prepped the patient. She found herself inching closer to the glass, her heart racing with anticipation. The tension in the room was palpable, but it wasn't fear—it was focus. The kind of intense focus that came from knowing you were about to change someone's life forever.

The surgery began with Dr. Martin making the initial incision. Amélie held her breath as the procedure unfolded before her, each movement precise and calculated. The room was silent except for the soft hum of the machines and the occasional instruction from Dr. Martin to her team.

Amélie's mind raced with questions, but she knew better than to ask them during the procedure. Instead, she mentally took note of everything she was witnessing—the tools, the techniques, the decision-making process. It was a masterclass in surgery, and Amélie was in awe of Dr. Martin's skill.

As the surgery progressed, Amélie found herself thinking about her own path. The last few months had been transformative in so many ways. She had thrown herself into her studies, spending long hours in the library and even longer nights working on her surgical equation. The equation had started as a simple idea—something to help surgeons predict outcomes more accurately—but it had grown into something much bigger.

Her equation, now nearly complete, was designed to revolutionize how surgeries were planned. By taking into account a patient's medical history, the complexity of the surgery, and potential complications, the formula could predict outcomes and help surgeons adjust their approach in real-time. It was a tool that could save lives, and Amélie was determined to perfect it.

But as much as she had thrown herself into her work, there was still a part of her that struggled to move past the grief of losing her grandfather. Alain had been her biggest supporter, always encouraging her to follow her dreams, and his absence still weighed heavily on her heart. There were days when the sorrow felt overwhelming, but lately, those days had been fewer and farther between.

Today, as she watched Dr. Martin expertly navigate the complexities of the surgery, Amélie felt something she hadn't felt in a long time: hope. The pain of her grandfather's loss would never fully disappear, but it was no longer the only thing she felt. There was room now for other emotions—joy, excitement, determination. It was as if she had turned a corner, and for the first time in months, Amélie felt like she was moving forward.

The surgery concluded successfully, and Dr. Martin stepped back from the operating table, her expression one of calm satisfaction. "Another successful outcome," she said, turning to Amélie. "What did you think?"

"It was incredible," Amélie replied, her voice full of admiration. "You made it look so easy."

Dr. Martin chuckled, removing her gloves. "It's never easy, but with enough practice, it becomes second nature. And one day, it'll be second nature for you too."

Amélie smiled, feeling a surge of confidence. "I hope so."

Amélie's Diary

Dear Diary,

It feels like the world is shifting, and somehow, I am too. Ever since I started my shadowing sessions at the hospital, I've been seeing things so differently. Not just the way surgeries are done, but also how life moves forward, how decisions are made, and how fragile everything truly is. There's a beauty in the fragility of life, something I've come to understand more and more these days.

Watching Dr. Martin perform surgery today, it felt like I was witnessing pure mastery. She was calm, collected, and entirely focused on the task in front of her. Every movement had purpose. I couldn't take my eyes off the operation, trying to take in every detail. It made me think about my own journey. I've always been fascinated by medicine, but seeing it up close like this, in the real world, makes it even more real. And in a way, it makes me feel closer to my dream of becoming a surgeon.

But there's something else I have to admit to you, Diary—I've been feeling different lately, like a part of me is changing, evolving. Maybe it's because of everything that's happened with Alain, maybe it's because I'm spending so much time at the hospital, or maybe it's just because I'm growing up. Either way, I feel like I'm stepping into a new version of myself. One that's more determined, more focused, but also one that carries a little more sorrow.

I miss Alain so much. I know I'll never stop missing him, but I also know he would want me to keep moving forward. And that's what I've been trying to do, though some days are harder than others. There are still moments when I feel like the sadness is too much, when I just want to crawl into bed and disappear under the covers. But then I remember how much Alain believed in me, and I find the strength to keep going.

There's something else I've been working on—something that's been keeping my mind busy. My equation. The one that I started a while ago, the one that I believe could change the way surgeries are done. I've refined it over the last few months, adding more variables, considering more outcomes. It's almost finished, and I really think it could help surgeons predict the outcomes of their procedures more accurately. I've kept it a secret for now. I'm not sure why, but it feels like something I need to hold close until it's ready.

I'm going to talk to Madame Laramie and Docteur Michel about it soon. They've been so supportive of me, not just academically but personally as well. They know about Alain and everything that's been going on in my family, and they've been so understanding. I don't think I'd be where I am without their support. But this equation—I want it to be perfect before I share it with them. It's a part of me now, something I've poured my heart and soul into.

Despite everything, I feel hopeful. It's strange, isn't it? To feel hope in the middle of sorrow. But I do. I feel like things are changing, and not just in the hospital or with my studies, but within me. It's like I'm on the edge of something big, something important. And as much as I'm nervous, I'm also excited to see where this new path leads me.

Even with all the pressure, the expectations, and the sadness, I feel stronger than I did before. Maybe that's what Alain wanted for me all along—to grow from this, to find my strength in the hardest moments. I think I'm finally starting to understand that.

À demain.

Amélie

Chapter 28: Rebuilding Trust

It had been weeks since Amélie's life took a drastic turn. The loss of Alain left a deep void in her heart, and despite all her efforts to focus on her dreams, it lingered like a cloud that never really lifted. She had begun her shadowing experience with Dr. Martin, learning the nuances of ENT surgery, something she felt deeply passionate about. But beyond the hospital and her studies, there was something else she needed to confront—trust.

There were fractures in her relationships, things left unsaid, and unresolved tensions that weighed on her. It wasn't just about the grief that came with losing Alain; it was about everything that had been set aside during that period. Her friendship with Alex had changed. Her relationship with Jasmine, even though it had improved, still held scars. And somewhere along the way, Amélie felt like she had lost a piece of herself in all the turmoil.

It was a cold winter morning when she woke up, determined to start the process of rebuilding what had been broken. She knew this wouldn't be easy, but she couldn't move forward without addressing the past.

Amélie sat down in the kitchen, her notebook open in front of her, but her thoughts drifted elsewhere. The smell of freshly brewed coffee filled the room as Jasmine entered, her soft footsteps barely audible. Amélie hadn't spoken to her aunt in depth since Alain's passing, despite the gradual thawing of their relationship.

"Ça va, Amélie?" Jasmine asked, her voice gentle but uncertain.

Amélie looked up and forced a small smile. "Oui, ça va. I was just thinking about... everything, I suppose." She paused, biting her lip. "Can we talk, Jasmine? Really talk?"

Jasmine hesitated for a moment, but then nodded. "Bien sûr."

They moved to the living room, where the fire crackled softly, warming the space. Amélie sat down on the couch, her hands fidgeting in her lap. This wasn't just about healing herself; it was about healing them.

"I want to talk about... us," Amélie began, her voice wavering slightly. "There's a lot that's happened. Between Alain, school, and everything else, I feel like we've never really addressed what went wrong."

Jasmine looked at her with soft eyes, guilt and remorse clouding her features. "I know I wasn't always fair to you, Amélie. I made mistakes—many of them. I didn't realize how much I hurt you until it was too late."

Amélie took a deep breath. "I know that. And I understand that you were going through things too, with your family and everything. But... I need to rebuild the trust between us. I want to forgive, but I also need to know that we're moving forward together."

Jasmine nodded, her eyes glistening. "I want that too, Amélie. I want to be someone you can count on, not just someone who was there in the background. I see how strong you've become, how you've persevered, and it makes me so proud. I know Alain would be proud too."

The mention of Alain's name brought a lump to Amélie's throat. She blinked back the tears and nodded. "I miss him every day. But I'm trying to honour his memory by living the life he'd want me to. That means fixing the things I can fix and letting go of what I can't."

Jasmine smiled softly, reaching over to take Amélie's hand. "We'll work on this, together. I promise."

For the first time in months, Amélie felt a sense of relief. A weight lifted from her chest, knowing that she and Jasmine were on the same page. It wasn't a perfect resolution, but it was a step in the right direction.

Later that day, Amélie headed to school. The cold air bit at her cheeks, but she welcomed the freshness. It cleared her mind as she thought about the next challenge she had to face—Alex.

Their relationship had always been complex. As her twin, Alex had always been by her side, but they had grown apart in recent months. He was focused on his own life, his football dreams taking precedence over everything else. And in turn, Amélie had thrown herself into her studies, her medical aspirations becoming her refuge.

She found him on the football field, practicing with his team. His movements were sharp and precise, his focus completely on the ball. Amélie stood on the sidelines, watching for a moment before calling out to him.

"Alex!" she shouted.

He turned, surprised to see her, but jogged over nonetheless. "Amélie? What's up?"

"I need to talk to you," she said simply.

Alex raised an eyebrow but nodded. "Sure, what's going on?"

They moved away from the field, walking toward the bleachers. Amélie took a deep breath, her mind racing as she tried to figure out where to start.

"I feel like we've been growing apart," she said finally. "I know we're both busy with our own lives, but I miss how we used to be. You've been distant, and I know I haven't been around as much either, but... I want to fix that."

Alex looked at her, his expression softening. "I've noticed it too. I guess I didn't know how to bring it up."

Amélie nodded. "We've both been through a lot. With Alain, with school, with everything. But I don't want to lose you, Alex. You're my twin, and that means something to me."

Alex sighed, running a hand through his hair. "It means something to me too. I guess I just didn't know how to handle everything. Football is my way of coping, and I've been using it as an escape. But that doesn't mean I don't care about you."

They stood in silence for a moment, the cold wind whipping around them. Then Alex spoke again.

"I'm sorry, Amélie. For not being there. For not noticing how much you were going through. I want to be better. I'll make more time for you, for us."

Amélie smiled, feeling a warmth spread through her chest. "Thank you. That's all I wanted."

As they walked back toward the field, Amélie felt lighter. It wasn't a perfect fix, but like with Jasmine, it was a step in the right direction. She was rebuilding the bridges that had been broken, and it felt good.

The next few days passed in a blur of schoolwork and hospital shadowing. Amélie threw herself into both, determined to excel in everything she did. Her equation for predicting surgical outcomes was still at the forefront of her mind, and she was getting closer to perfecting it. She just needed the right moment to share it with Madame Laramie and Docteur Michel.

When the time finally came, Amélie sat down with them in the science lab, her nerves buzzing with anticipation.

"Amélie, what's on your mind?" Madame Laramie asked, her kind eyes focused on Amélie.

"I've been working on something," Amélie began, pulling out her notebook. "It's an equation. One that I think could revolutionize surgery. It's designed to help surgeons predict outcomes more accurately and adjust their techniques accordingly."

Docteur Michel leaned forward, her interest piqued. "That sounds intriguing. Can you walk us through it?"

Amélie nodded, her hands trembling slightly as she opened her notebook to the correct page. She explained the equation in detail, outlining how it worked, the variables involved, and how it could be applied in a clinical setting.

By the time she finished, both Madame Laramie and Docteur Michel were silent, their expressions thoughtful.

"Amélie, this is... incredible," Madame Laramie said finally. "You've thought of everything. This could genuinely make a difference in the medical field."

Docteur Michel nodded in agreement. "I'm impressed, Amélie. You have a brilliant mind, and this equation is a testament to that."

Amélie's heart swelled with pride. "Thank you. I've been working on it for months, but I didn't feel ready to share it until now."

"You should be proud of yourself," Madame Laramie said. "And we're here to support you, in whatever way you need."

Amélie smiled, feeling a sense of accomplishment wash over her. For the first time in a long time, she felt like things were finally falling into place. She had rebuilt trust with her family, she had found her footing at the hospital, and now she had something concrete to show for all her hard work.

It wasn't the end of her journey—far from it. But it was a new beginning, one that filled her with hope for the future.

Amélie's Diary

Dear Diary,

Today feels different. Not in a monumental, earth-shattering way, but in a quiet, subtle way, like a small shift in the wind. I woke up this morning feeling lighter, like a burden I hadn't even realized I was carrying had been lifted off my shoulders. Maybe it's because I'm finally starting to rebuild the trust that had been shattered over the past few months, or maybe it's because I'm learning to accept that not everything can be fixed in a day, or even in a week. But progress... it feels like progress.

I had a real heart-to-heart with Jasmine today. It's strange, isn't it? How things have changed between us. There was a time when I couldn't stand the sight of her, when every word out of her mouth felt like a dagger aimed straight at me. But I guess grief does strange things to people. It warps your perception, makes you see things that aren't there, or worse, makes you miss the things that are right in front of you.

She apologized today. And not just a passing "sorry" like before. It felt real, sincere, like she finally understood the weight of everything. She admitted her mistakes, how she hadn't been there for me, how she had let her own issues cloud her judgment. And you know what? It was hard. It was hard to hear her say those things because a part of me didn't want to forgive her. A part of me wanted to hold onto the anger, the resentment. But that's not who I want to be. I don't want to be weighed down by bitterness.

I told her that I needed to rebuild the trust between us, that it would take time. And she agreed. She's willing to put in the effort, and for that, I'm grateful. It doesn't erase the past, but it gives me hope for the future. For the first time in a long time, I feel like we're on the same page.

And then there's Alex. Talking to him was probably the hardest part of today. We've been drifting apart for months, and I guess I didn't even realize how much I missed him until I saw him on the football field today. He was so focused, so in his element, and for a moment, I felt like I didn't even know him anymore. But when we talked, I realized that he had been feeling the same way. We've both been so wrapped up in our own worlds—me with my studies and the hospital, him with football—that we forgot how to be there for each other.

He apologized too, which surprised me. Alex isn't the type to admit when he's wrong, but today, he did. He said he's going to try harder, make more time for me, for us. And that means the world to me. I've always looked up to Alex, even when we were fighting. He's my twin, my other half, and I don't want to lose that bond.

So, all in all, it's been a day of rebuilding. Rebuilding trust, rebuilding relationships, and maybe even rebuilding myself. I've spent so much time trying to be strong, to push through the pain, that I didn't realize how much I needed to stop and heal.

And then there's the hospital. Oh, Diary, I can't even begin to describe how much shadowing Dr. Martin has meant to me. ENT surgery is everything I hoped it would be and more. Every day I learn something new, something exciting. I feel like I'm exactly where I'm supposed to be. And today, I finally shared my equation with Madame Laramie and Docteur Michel.

I was so nervous, Diary. I had been working on this equation for months, tweaking it, perfecting it, but I wasn't sure if it was ready. But they were both so supportive, so encouraging. They actually seemed impressed! Madame Laramie said it could revolutionize surgery, and Docteur Michel said it had the potential to make a real difference in the field. Hearing that from them... it was everything I needed.

It's funny, isn't it? How the things that seemed so impossible just a few months ago now feel within reach. There was a time when I thought I'd never be able to focus on my studies again, that the weight of everything would crush me. But here I am, not just surviving, but thriving. And I think Alain would be proud of me. I hope he would be.

I miss him, Diary. Every single day, I miss him. But I'm learning to live with the grief, to carry it with me without letting it consume me. It's part of who I am now, part of my story, but it's not the whole story. I have so much more ahead of me, so many things I want to do, and I know I can't let the past hold me back. Alain wouldn't want that. He'd want me to live, to succeed, to be happy.

So that's what I'm going to do. I'm going to keep moving forward, one step at a time. I'm going to rebuild my relationships, work on my studies, and continue shadowing Dr. Martin. And who knows? Maybe one day, I'll be the surgeon who uses my own equation to save lives.

But for now, I'm just taking it one day at a time. And today was a good day.

Amélie

Chapter 29: Embracing the Future

The early morning sun cast a soft golden hue over the city as Amélie stood on the balcony of her room, sipping her tea. It had been several months since Alain's passing, and although the pain still lingered, the healing process had made way for new beginnings. Winter had slowly given way to spring, and with it, a renewed sense of hope. The flowers were beginning to bloom, and the air was filled with the promise of change.

Amélie's heart was a mix of apprehension and excitement as she prepared for another significant chapter in her life. Today marked the day she would present her revolutionary surgical equation to a panel of esteemed surgeons and medical researchers at a conference. This was a huge step for her—one that could potentially shape her future in ways she had only dreamed of.

Alex, who had been incredibly supportive despite their occasional sibling spats, was by her side. They had grown closer over the past few months, finding solace in each other's company and supporting one another through the trials and triumphs. He offered a reassuring smile as they entered the conference hall together.

"Ready for this?" Alex asked, adjusting his tie.

"Not really," Amélie admitted with a nervous laugh. "But I guess I have to be."

They were greeted by the buzz of excitement in the conference hall. It was filled with medical professionals from around the world, each eager to hear the latest innovations in their field. Amélie's presentation was scheduled to be one of the highlights of the morning session, and she could feel the weight of anticipation pressing down on her.

As the time for her presentation drew closer, Amélie took a deep breath and reviewed her notes one last time. Her equation, which she had spent countless hours developing, was designed to predict surgical outcomes and adjust procedures in real-time, thus potentially revolutionizing the way surgeries were conducted. It was her way of honouring Alain's memory—by making a tangible difference in the world, just as he had always inspired her to do.

The moment arrived, and Amélie took the stage, her heart pounding in her chest. She glanced at the audience, spotting familiar faces—Madame Laramie, Docteur Michel, and even Dr. Martin, who had supported her throughout her journey. Their presence filled her with a sense of calm, knowing she had a strong support system.

"Good morning, everyone," she began, her voice steady but filled with a hint of nervousness. "My name is Amélie Dubois, and today I am presenting my equation designed to enhance surgical precision and predict outcomes."

The presentation began, and Amélie delved into the complexities of her work, explaining how her equation could help surgeons adjust their techniques during operations based on real-time data. She spoke passionately about the potential impact this could have on patient outcomes and the future of surgical practices.

The audience listened intently, and as Amélie concluded her presentation, a wave of relief washed over her. She had done it. She had shared her vision with the world, and the feedback she received was overwhelmingly positive.

Madame Laramie and Docteur Michel approached her after the presentation, their faces beaming with pride.

"Amélie, that was extraordinary," Madame Laramie said, embracing her. "Your dedication and hard work have truly paid off."

Docteur Michel nodded in agreement. "You have a brilliant future ahead of you, Amélie. Your work has the potential to change lives, and I am excited to see where it leads."

As the conference continued, Amélie felt a deep sense of fulfilment. The validation of her work was a significant milestone, but more importantly, it symbolized her ability to overcome the challenges she had faced. It was a testament to her resilience and determination.

Later that evening, Amélie and Alex walked through the city, enjoying the warm spring breeze. The day had been a whirlwind, but now it was time to reflect and celebrate.

"Today was incredible," Alex said, his eyes twinkling with pride. "You did amazing."

Amélie smiled, feeling a mix of gratitude and contentment. "Thank you for being here with me, Alex. It means a lot."

They continued walking, discussing the day's events and their future plans. For Amélie, this was more than just a successful presentation; it was a step towards embracing a future she had once only dreamed of. savour

As the sun set and the stars began to twinkle in the sky, Amélie felt a profound sense of peace. She knew that life would continue to bring its challenges, but she also knew that she had the strength and support to face them. Her journey was far from over, but she was ready to embrace whatever came next with hope and determination.

This was her moment—her chance to build a future that honoured the past while forging ahead with courage and optimism. And with each step she took, she felt more prepared to face the adventures that lay ahead.

For now, though, Amélie allowed herself to savour the success of the day and the promise of the future. She was ready for whatever came next, knowing that she had the strength, the support, and the unwavering belief in herself to make a difference.

And as she looked up at the night sky, she couldn't help but smile, knowing that her journey was just beginning.

Amélie's Diary

Dear Diary,

Today was a significant day, and I feel a mix of emotions as I reflect on everything that happened. The conference was an enormous milestone for me. I've spent so much time working on my equation, and finally presenting it felt like a dream come true. The feedback was overwhelmingly positive, and it's reassuring to know that my work has the potential to make a real difference in the world.

When I stood on that stage, I felt a wave of nerves crashing over me, but once I started speaking, I found my rhythm. I looked out into the audience and saw familiar faces—Madame Laramie, Docteur Michel, and Dr. Martin. Their support meant the world to me, and their smiles helped calm my jitters. It felt so good to share my passion with people who truly understand and appreciate the impact of what I've been working on.

Alex was with me the entire day, and his presence was a source of comfort and strength. We spent the evening walking through the city, talking about the day and our plans for the future. It was such a relief to unwind and share these moments with him. It's moments like these that remind me of how fortunate I am to have such supportive family and friends.

Despite the happiness of today, there's still a part of me that feels the weight of Alain's absence. I miss him so much, and I often wonder how he would have reacted to everything that's happening now. I find solace in knowing that I'm doing something meaningful, something that I hope would make him proud. It's my way of keeping his memory alive and honouring his legacy.

There's still a lot to do, and I know that the road ahead will have its challenges. But today, I felt a renewed sense of hope and purpose. The positive feedback on my equation has given me the motivation to keep pushing forward and continue working towards my goals. I'm excited about the possibilities and the future that lies ahead.

It's been a while since Alain passed away, and while the pain of his loss is still there, I'm learning to embrace the changes and find a new sense of normalcy. Each day is a step towards healing and finding joy again, and today was a significant part of that journey.

I'm looking forward to the future and the opportunities it will bring. There's a lot to look forward to, and I'm ready to face whatever comes next with optimism and determination. For now, I'm going to savour the success of today and take comfort in the support of those around me.

As I sit here and reflect, I'm reminded of the importance of staying true to myself and my dreams. Today was a reminder that even in the face of adversity, there's always a chance for growth and new beginnings.

Until next time,

Amélie

Chapter 30: The Heart Remembers

The evening sun dipped low on the horizon, casting a warm, golden glow over the city of Nice. The air was crisp, and the shadows of the buildings stretched long across the streets. Amélie walked slowly through the familiar pathways of her neighborhood, her thoughts a swirl of emotion as she made her way home. Today marked a poignant moment—a memorial in honour of her grandfather, Alain. Despite the passage of time, his absence was felt deeply, and this evening was dedicated to remembering the impact he had on their lives.

As Amélie approached her family home, she noticed the changes that had been made to prepare for the memorial. The front yard was adorned with an array of white and yellow flowers, arranged meticulously in memory of Alain. Soft, ambient lights illuminated the walkway, guiding guests toward the entrance. The house itself had been transformed into a sanctuary of remembrance, with gentle lighting casting a warm, inviting glow over the interior.

Inside, the atmosphere was serene and reflective. The living room had been elegantly decorated with photographs of Alain, each framed beautifully and arranged in a way that told the story of his life. Amélie paused for a moment to take in the sight—images of Alain smiling, laughing, and sharing cherished moments with family and friends. It was a visual tapestry of the love and joy he had brought into their lives.

Marie, Alain's widow, was at the heart of the preparations. Her presence, though marked by an evident sadness, exuded a quiet strength. Marie had put considerable effort into creating a space that honoured Alain's memory and allowed everyone to come together in celebration of his life. She moved through the room with grace, her eyes occasionally moistening as she prepared for the evening.

Amélie's brother, Alex, greeted her with a somber smile. "Hey, Amélie," he said softly, his voice carrying the weight of their shared grief. "Are you ready for tonight?"

Amélie nodded, her heart heavy with a mix of sorrow and anticipation. "I think so. It feels like just yesterday we were talking about him. I've been reflecting on everything he meant to us."

Alex placed a reassuring hand on her shoulder. "We'll get through this together. It's important that we remember him and celebrate the wonderful person he was."

The memorial began with Marie taking center stage. Her voice, though choked with emotion, conveyed the profound love she had for Alain. She spoke of their years together, their shared experiences, and the ways in which Alain had touched the lives of everyone around him. Her tribute was heartfelt and poignant, capturing the essence of the man they had all admired and loved.

As Marie spoke, Amélie's thoughts drifted back to the many conversations she had had with Alain. He had always been a source of wisdom and encouragement, and his belief in her had been unwavering. She remembered the times he had guided her through difficult moments, offering advice and comfort. Alain's presence had been a constant source of strength, and his absence left a void that was still deeply felt.

After Marie's tribute, guests began to share their own memories of Alain. The room was filled with murmurs of affection and admiration as people recounted anecdotes about his generosity, humour, and the positive impact he had on their lives. Each story painted a picture of a man who had left an indelible mark on those around him.

Amélie listened intently, her heart swelling with a mixture of pride and sadness. She was moved by the outpouring of love and respect for her grandfather. The stories not only highlighted Alain's qualities but also underscored the deep connections he had forged with everyone he met.

As the evening continued, Amélie found solace in the shared memories and the presence of her family and friends. The conversations, the laughter, and the collective reflection on Alain's life provided a sense of comfort. The support of those around her was a reminder that even in the face of loss, there was strength to be found in unity and shared experiences.

The night grew colder, and the air outside became brisk. Amélie stepped out into the garden, seeking a moment of solitude. The sky above was a tapestry of stars, and the gentle breeze rustled the leaves of the trees. She took a deep breath, allowing the tranquillity of the night to wash over her.

Sitting on a bench in the garden, Amélie closed her eyes and let her mind wander through the memories of her grandfather. She could almost hear his voice, offering words of wisdom and encouragement. The memories were a source of comfort, a reminder of the love and guidance Alain had provided throughout her life.

As she sat there, Amélie felt a sense of connection to Alain. It was as if his spirit was present, whispering reassurances and reminding her of the strength he had instilled in her. The night was filled with a quiet peace, and Amélie found herself reflecting on the legacy Alain had left behind.

The stars above seemed to twinkle in acknowledgment of the memories and emotions Amélie was experiencing. She thought about how Alain had always encouraged her to pursue her dreams and to face challenges with resilience. His belief in her had been unwavering, and she felt a renewed sense of purpose as she considered the path ahead.

Eventually, Amélie made her way back inside, where the warmth of the house offered a contrast to the chill of the night. The memorial had been a meaningful and emotional experience, and she felt a sense of closure. The love and support of her family and friends had been a source of strength, and she was grateful for the opportunity to honour Alain's memory.

As the evening ended, Amélie took one last look at the photographs and mementos that celebrated her grandfather's life. Each image, each memory, was a testament to the man he had been and the impact he had made. She knew that while Alain was no longer physically present, his spirit would continue to guide and inspire her.

With a final glance at the stars, Amélie headed back to her room. The night had been a tribute to a remarkable man, and she was grateful for the love and support that had surrounded her. As she settled into bed, she felt a sense of calm and closure. The heart remembers, and in those memories, she found peace and strength.

Epilogue: Twenty Years Later

The winter sun cast a gentle glow over the snow-covered streets of Geneva as Amélie Morel and her family arrived in the city. The picturesque scenery, with its glistening snow and the majestic backdrop of the Alps, set the stage for a heartfelt reunion. Geneva, with its blend of Swiss charm and cosmopolitan flair, was the perfect location for this long-awaited family gathering.

Amélie, now known as Amélie Morel, had built a successful life in London. As a renowned ENT surgeon, her expertise was well-regarded in the UK. She had earned a reputation for her innovative approaches and compassionate care. Her dedication to her field had not only brought her professional acclaim but also personal fulfilment. Amélie's husband, Pierre Morel, was an accomplished architect whose designs had garnered significant praise in London's competitive market. Together, they were a power couple, balancing their demanding careers while nurturing a loving family life.

Their children, Lucas, eight, and Camille, five, were excited about the trip to Geneva. Lucas, with his inquisitive nature, was eager to explore the new city and learn about its history. Camille, with her cheerful disposition, was thrilled at the prospect of meeting her extended family and making new friends. Amélie and Pierre had prepared them for the reunion, explaining the significance of reconnecting with their roots and celebrating family ties.

Alex Dubois, Amélie's brother, had embarked on a different journey since their last meeting. His football career had reached great heights, earning him fame and admiration in Spain. Alongside his wife, Julie Blanchet, an accomplished artist, Alex had found a new home in sunny Spain. Julie's artwork had flourished in the vibrant Spanish art scene, while Alex continued to excel in his football career. Their daughters, Isabelle and Élise, added joy to their lives, making the move to Spain a new chapter filled with opportunities.

The reunion in Geneva was a significant event, bringing together family members from across Europe. Amélie had meticulously planned the gathering, ensuring that every detail was perfect. She had booked tickets for her immediate family, Alex and his family, as well as for their parents, Isabelle and François. The occasion was not only a celebration of their individual achievements but also a cherished opportunity to reconnect with Amélie's maternal side of the family.

As Amélie's family arrived at the venue, they were greeted by the elegant charm of the Swiss city. The venue was a beautifully decorated hall, adorned with a blend of French and Swiss elements, reflecting the cultural richness of the gathering. Soft lights and festive decorations created a warm and inviting atmosphere, setting the stage for an evening of reconnection and celebration.

Claire, Amélie's aunt, and her husband, Charles, were among the first to welcome the arriving guests. Claire, with her nurturing demeanour, expressed her pride in Amélie's accomplishments and eagerly embraced her niece. Charles, known for his wit and warmth, shared fond memories of past family gatherings. The reunion was also an opportunity for Claire and Charles to catch up with Alex and his family, exchanging stories and updates on their lives.

Juliet and Nicolas, Amélie's maternal grandparents, were thrilled to see their granddaughter and her family. Juliet, with her gracious presence, greeted Amélie with tears of joy, while Nicolas, with his wise and gentle demeanour, offered words of encouragement and pride. The reunion with Juliet and Nicolas was particularly special for Amélie, as it provided a chance to reconnect with her roots and share her achievements with those who had supported her throughout her life.

As the evening progressed, the venue came alive with conversation and laughter. The families gathered around elegantly set tables, enjoying a delightful mix of French and Swiss cuisine. The menu featured dishes that reflected the cultural blend of the gathering, from savoury fondue to delicate pastries. The meal was a celebration of both the family's heritage and their shared experiences.

During dinner, Amélie and Alex took time to reflect on their journeys. They reminisced about their childhood, the challenges they had faced, and the support they had received from their family. Amélie shared stories of her career in London, highlighting the milestones she had achieved and the impact she had made in the field of ENT surgery. Alex spoke about his football career, the joys of living in Spain, and the excitement of watching his daughters grow.

The conversation flowed easily, with family members switching between French and English as they caught up on each other's lives. The children played together, their laughter and excitement adding to the festive atmosphere. Isabelle and Élise quickly bonded with Lucas and Camille, their playful interactions a testament to the strength of family connections.

As the night continued, Amélie and Pierre took a moment to express their gratitude for the reunion. They were thankful for the opportunity to reconnect with their extended family and celebrate their shared achievements. The event was a reminder of the importance of family ties and the joy of coming together to celebrate life's milestones.

The evening concluded with a group photo, capturing the essence of the reunion. The photo showcased the unity and love that bound the family together, a visual reminder of the cherished moments they had shared. The group's smiles and laughter were a testament to the strength of their relationships and the joy they found in each other's company.

As the night drew to a close, the families bid farewell and prepared to return to their respective homes. Amélie, Alex, and their families left Geneva with hearts full of gratitude and joy. The memories of the reunion would remain a source of inspiration and strength as they continued to embrace the future, knowing they had a supportive and loving family to share it with.

Amélie and her family returned to London, where they continued to thrive in their lives and careers. Alex and his family settled back into their life in Spain, cherishing the memories of their time in Geneva. The reunion had strengthened their bonds and provided them with a renewed sense of connection and support.

The journey from Geneva had been a meaningful and enriching experience for everyone involved. It had reaffirmed the importance of family and the joy of coming together to celebrate their shared history and achievements. As they moved forward, Amélie, Alex, and their families carried with them the memories of a special reunion, a reminder of the love and support that had always been a part of their lives.

Amélie's Diary

Dear Diary,

As I sit here reflecting on the past few days, I feel an overwhelming sense of joy and fulfilment. Our recent trip to Geneva was a dream come true, and I'm grateful for every moment we shared.

Seeing my mother's side of the family again was truly special. Juliet and Nicolas, my beloved grandparents, greeted us with their characteristic warmth and affection. Their love and wisdom have always been a cornerstone in my life, and reconnecting with them felt like coming home. Juliet's embrace and Nicolas's comforting presence reminded me of the strength and support they've given me throughout my life.

Claire and Charles, my aunt and uncle, were just as wonderful as I remembered. Claire's kindness and Charles's humour made our time together so enjoyable. Catching up with them and sharing our experiences brought back so many fond memories. Their pride in Alex and me was heartwarming, and their support continues to mean the world to us.

Alex, Julie, and their two beautiful daughters, Isabelle and Elise, joined us for the trip. Seeing them together and witnessing their happiness was a joy. Isabelle, at 5 years old, was full of energy and curiosity, while Elise, just 2, brought her own kind of sweet charm to the family gathering. It was wonderful to see Alex with his family and to experience their joy and excitement firsthand.

Pierre and I were thrilled to introduce our children, Lucas and Camille, to their extended family. Lucas, our 8-year-old, was fascinated by all the new experiences and enjoyed every moment of meeting his cousins. Camille, our 5-year-old, was equally excited and made fast friends with Isabelle and Elise. Watching them play together and seeing the joy in their faces was a highlight of the trip.

Our time in Geneva was more than just a family reunion; it was a moment of reflection and gratitude. From the challenges we've faced to the milestones we've achieved, it's been an incredible journey. I'm thankful for the love and support we've received from everyone around us, which has helped us navigate life's ups and downs with resilience and grace.

As I look to the future, I feel optimistic and hopeful. The road hasn't always been easy, but with the unwavering support of our loved ones and the strength we've found within ourselves, we've managed to overcome obstacles and find joy in the journey.

With Pierre by my side and our beautiful children, Lucas and Camille, our lives are filled with love and laughter. I'm grateful for the family we've built and the new memories we continue to create.

Here's to new beginnings and the bright future that lies ahead.

Amélie

Acknowledgements

Writing this book has been a profound journey of reflection, creativity, and personal growth. I would like to extend my heartfelt gratitude to everyone who has been a part of this journey, making it possible for me to share this story with the world.

First and foremost, I want to express my deepest thanks to my family. Your unwavering support, encouragement, and love have been the cornerstone of my strength throughout this endeavour. A special thank you to my parents, whose sacrifices and belief in me have shaped the person I am today. Your guidance and inspiration have been invaluable.

I would also like to extend my gratitude to my teachers, whose wisdom and encouragement have nurtured my love for writing and storytelling. Your dedication to fostering creativity and critical thinking has profoundly impacted my work and my life.

To my friends, thank you for your support and for standing by me through the highs and lows of this journey. Your presence and belief in me have been a source of comfort and motivation.

I am immensely grateful to my supporters, whose encouragement and enthusiasm have fuelled my passion for writing. Your positive feedback and kind words have been a great source of inspiration.

A big thank you to the publishing companies who believed in this project and provided the platform for this book to come to life. Your expertise and support have been crucial in bringing my vision to fruition.

I must extend the biggest thanks to my family, especially my parents, for being my rock throughout this process. Your endless love and support have been my guiding light.

Lastly, I want to offer a profound and heartfelt thanks to my late grandfather, Balasubramaniam. Even though a part of me was torn away with his passing, his belief in me and his enduring presence in my memories continue to inspire me. He will forever remain in my heart and live on through the stories and memories we shared.

In creating Amélie Dubois, I chose to draw deeply from my own experiences and emotions. Although the family dynamics and names have been altered for the sake of narrative, Amélie's journey reflects my own path—marked by trials, growth, and the relentless pursuit of dreams. This book is a tribute to the strength and resilience that we all carry within us, and it is my hope that Amélie's story resonates with readers on a deeply personal level.

Thank you to everyone who has been a part of this journey. Your support has made this book possible, and I am forever grateful.

With heartfelt appreciation,

Danika Prasad

Also by Danika Prasad

Once Upon Historians
Meanwhile, Elsewhere
Invitation to Paris

About the Author

Danika, a 13-year-old bookworm, has always been passionate about reading and writing. As she delved deeper into her studies, her love for learning only grew stronger. She spent hours devouring books of all genres, and soon discovered that she had a knack for storytelling herself. With the encouragement of her teachers and family, Danika began writing her own tales, weaving intricate plots and characters that came alive on the page. Her hard work paid off when she published her first book, "Once Upon Historians", a historical fiction novel that combines her love of reading and learning. Through writing, Danika finds solace and escape from the stresses of everyday life, using her words as a tool to cope with her emotions and process her thoughts. With "Once Upon Historians" under her belt, Danika is determined to continue pursuing her dreams and inspiring others to do the same. Danika, a 13-year-old bookworm, has always been passionate about reading and writing. As she delved deeper into her studies, her love for learning only grew stronger. She spent hours devouring books of all genres, and soon discovered that she had a knack for storytelling herself. With the encouragement of her teachers and family, Danika began writing her own tales, weaving intricate plots and characters that came alive on the page. Her hard work paid off when she published her first book, "Once Upon Historians", a historical fiction novel that combines her love of reading and learning. Through writing, Danika finds solace and escape from the stresses of everyday life, using her words as a tool to cope with her emotions and process her thoughts. With "Once Upon Historians" under her belt, Danika is determined to continue pursuing her dreams and inspiring others to do the same.

Milton Keynes UK
Ingram Content Group UK Ltd.
UKHW021840231124
451423UK00001B/154

9 798227 806079